Before the Thin Man

The Prequel to Dashiell Hammett's *The Thin Man*

Christopher Allen

This novel's story and characters are fictitious and any similarities to real persons, living or deceased, are purely coincidental. Although certain long standing institutions, businesses, agencies, and public offices may be mentioned, the characters involved and story are wholly imaginary.

For Linda

1

I was sitting at my regular table at a speakeasy on Fifty-Second Street waiting to meet up with Clyde Wynant. He called me earlier in the week telling me something about a business deal gone sour, and his new business partner running aground. He wanted to see me to consult about his options and learn what he should already know about his new colleague. I don't usually get involved in these sort of matters but I've known Clyde for some time and he's a good customer. I tried to tell him on the phone he would probably be wasting his time and money and just bail out of this thing while he could. His lawyer, Herbert Macauley, was going to meet with us too. He's an old army buddy of mine from the war and has brought me plenty of business with several of his other clients. My bourbon arrived by the time Clyde had walked in and took off his coat and hat. He walked over when I waved and as he pulled his chair out, I sampled my drink.

"Nick, how've you been?"

"I can't complain Clyde. Especially now that my drink order came out. What are you having?"

"Did Macauley fill you in?"

"More or less."

"Good. I'll try to fill in the details without taking up the rest of your day."

"Slow down Clyde, we're not in that much of a hurry. What are you drinking?"

"What are you having?"

"Bourbon."

"Sounds good to me." he said.

"Neat, with water, soda, any particular pedigree?"

"Just the same as you, thanks."
I waved over to the bartender and raised my glass letting them know to send over another.

"So, how did this start?" I asked.

"Well, you know about some of my projects. Mostly in metallurgy and precious metals smelting and alloying processes."

"Well, sort of."

"Anyway, I was working on a project using silver in a photographic process-" he said. After a short pause he restarted. "Never mind all that. To make a long story short, I was working on a new thing for the dental field using radiation to image patients' mouths. It basically miniaturizes the photographic plate so it will fit in the mouth. The main thing I was working on is the silver based emulsion used in the slide."

"Okay," I said, not really clear about what he was going on about.

"A Chicago dentist by the name of Dwight Rosewood called me not too long ago. He told me he read about my experiments in the science and trade journals and wanted to contact me about trial runs and possibly partnering with me as a consultant, and with financing too. I thought it sounded like a good idea at the time."

"I take it, it wasn't such a good idea after all."

"You take it right."

"Clyde, did you do any checking on this guy before you got in too deep?"

"Well, you see—"

"That's what I thought. You know you can't just jump into things like this."

As Clyde began to explain further I noticed Macauley at the door. He was checking his coat and hat. Then I saw Mimi walk in and start yipping at him like an angry Chihuahua. It was apparent this confrontation had started outside and she followed him in refusing to be ignored. All I could think of was 'Poor Man'. I said to Wynant, "Never mind right now."

"What?"

"Look Clyde, you've got to go. And I mean now."

"What!?"

"Mimi just walked in and she's got Macauley cornered. She must have stalked him and followed him in. They didn't walk in together." I leaned in close. "She must be hunting you."

"I'm not running from her."

"Yes you are. We don't have time for your house keeping troubles and quite frankly, I'm not sticking around to watch you two dance around the May Pole. I don't care how many girlfriends you have or boyfriends she has, or vice versa, and I sure don't want to sit here and listen to you two go over it. If you want to talk to me and Mac go duck in the men's room now. When we get rid of her we'll get you. Then we'll finish our real business here."

"Alright" he said as he glanced back in her direction and eased his chair back from the table. He seemed to strain to walk slowly and blend with the other patrons as he egressed toward the end of the bar.

As Clyde slinked off one way Macauley approached from the other. Mimi still nipping at Mac's heels. She was so wound up and snapping at Mac she never noticed Clyde making his retreat. As they approached I stood and extended a hand. "Herbert… Herbert Macauley, it's good to see you again. How've you been?"

"Well, hello Nick. Small world bumping into you here."

"Yes, isn't it?" I said. "Won't you pull up a chair?"

Mimi stood quiet now but was shooting daggers at me with her eyes. "Well if it isn't Nick Charles. Aren't you going to say anything to me?"

"Why?"

"Oh! I never!" she huffed.

"Oh yes Mimi, you have too," I replied.

"I will not stand here and be insulted like that," she said, crossing her arms.

"Well then Mimi, bye."

She stomped one foot on the floor, spun on her heels, and stormed back out the front door. As she made her way off, Herbert and I settled back into our chairs.

"Thanks for rescuing me Nick."

"Think nothing of it. I'm glad she's gone too. What did Clyde ever see in that woman?"

"Where is he?"

"I gave him an early warning and he ducked out. I told him we would get him out of the men's room when the coast was clear. What are you drinking?"

"What are you having?"

"Bourbon."

"Sounds good to me," he said.

I waved over to the bar and raised my glass letting them know to send over yet another, only this time I raised two fingers. I needed a refill. "We'll let Clyde sweat it out for a minute. Serves him right for getting us in the middle of his headache."

"You must mean nightmare. Besides that, there's another client I wanted to talk with you about anyway. I think I need your help on this one too."

"Okay, fire away."

"We really don't have the time to go into here like I need to," he said. "For now I guess we really should get Wynant out of the men's room. Call my office and have Miss Jacobs set up a meeting. That way we won't be bothered by other things and I can go over it with you without distractions."

"I guess you're right."

"When do you think you can you drop by?"

"You name it Mac. I can always work you in."

"Will do. Do you think we should get Clyde back out here?"

I raised my glass, half hearing him, and was somewhat dreading getting Clyde. Knowing how he is I wasn't sure what tales he had in store for us. "I'll go get him. You enjoy the drink for a peaceful minute. Then we'll listen to the old bird beat his gums again."

Sticking my head in the men's room I called out, "Clyde!"

"Is she gone?" he asked as he emerged from a stall.

"Come on Clyde. Let's go back out to the table. Mac's waiting on us."

"Okay."

When we finally got settled in I asked Clyde to fill us in on his situation again. "Okay, now tell us about this Rosewood fella. You said he was a doctor?"

"He's a dentist."

"Right."

"He phoned my office several weeks ago from Chicago. He left a message with Julia-"

"Julia? Julia Wolf? Is she still around?"

Macauley interjected, "She's Clyde's secretary now."

"Oh, I see. That's what we're calling it these days?"

"I thought you didn't care about—"

"I don't Clyde. Go ahead with your story."

"Anyway, he left a message with her saying he was interested in my project. When I finally found the time to call him back he verified knowing

10

about my work from reading the journals. Looking back on it, I can't remember anyone talking with me about it for such an article. But I can't keep up with all that sort of stuff."

"They probably didn't. This is starting to sound just a little fishy to me already."

Clyde went on for a little while longer running the story down to us until he got to the part where Rosewood said he was going to bomb his house and kill his family.

"Did you report this to the police, Clyde?" I asked.

"Well, no. I didn't think they would believe me. Or it would do any good."

"That may be, but you still should have let them know something. It, at least, needs to be on record. I know blowing up houses is no big deal but letting somebody know might help a little."

"I guess you're right."

"If something did happen they'd at least have somewhere to start looking."

"I see your point."

"Look Clyde, you go down to the Precinct near your shop and get someone to write this up. Me and Mac will figure out what we need to do on our end, alright?"

As he stood, he said, "Thanks Charles, I'll go ahead and get that done," as he shook hands with Mac and me.

"We'll be talking soon. Take care Clyde."

Wynant made his way back out the door and Macauley and I sat back down.

"So Mac, what's your take?"

"There could be something to this. The world is full of confidence men, you know."

"Yeah. There is definitely no shortage of grifters. Hey, do you know anything about that so-called accountant Clyde's got working for him? That, ah, ah-"

"Tanner. His name is Tanner."

"That's right. Tanner. What's his story?" I asked.

"I'm not sure where he originally comes from, but he does have a bit of a record. And that secretary he's taken on is no prize either."

"The Wolf girl? He's been seeing her on the side for a while."

"Yeah. Julia Wolf. I'm not sure that's even her real name."

"I'm not either. What does Mimi think of all this monkey business? I mean, are they still under the same roof?"

"I think she's already kicked him out. Not sure."

"Oh, really. Wow. I didn't think that would ever happen. They love to fight."

"They're still married but I don't know for how much longer."

"I guess Julia's talents extend beyond typing and making coffee to rate getting hired. Clyde doesn't need a secretary. He's got Tanner working in the office."

"I wouldn't be surprised to find out if Tanner or Julia knows this Rosewood guy and they're setting Clyde up. Or Tanner and Julia are both in it with Rosewood."

"Clyde might eventually link Tanner to Rosewood, if they are working together, and it's not too late. But, he's not too bright when it comes to a smiling pretty face. I'm guessing Mimi knows this all too well too."

"It would seem. She tries to use the same tricks, but with much less effect. And she's just about the most incessant and garrulous women I've ever known."

"You really don't like her, do you?"

"What gave it away?"

2

I finally made it to Macauley's office around ten
Wednesday morning. Everyone knows Mondays are
a bad day for new business, with all the filings and
pleadings, and posting bonds. It's catch up day from
the weekend. And Tuesday isn't much better. That's
the day everybody is double checking what they did
on Monday. So Wednesdays work for me.
Sometimes I wonder why Macauley struck out on
his own. When he worked at the firm life was much
easier for him. Oh, now I remember. Money.

"Mr. Macauley will see you now," his
secretary said almost as soon as I closed the door
behind me.

I said, "Thanks," as I walked past her desk
to his door.

"Nick, how are you this fine morning?" he
asked as I entered.

"Fine Mac, just fine. You're awfully
cheerful today."

"Coffee?"

"Please."

Macauley leaned into his phone on the desk
and pressed a lever. "Miss Jacobs?"

"Yes sir?" came her voice over the speaker.

"Would you bring Mr. Charles a cup of coffee? Black please."

"Yes sir."

I hung my hat and overcoat on the tree next to the door and took my usual seat across the desk from him. Macauley slid some papers into a drawer and looked up. "Thanks for coming Nick. I'm afraid I really will need your help on this one."

"So what is it? Not Clyde again I hope."

"You can relax. No."

"Thanks."

"Here's a dollar," he said as he opened his wallet. "You've been retained. Now I'll fill you in."

"Alright. It's official. Go ahead."

"Have you heard of Consolidated Transcontinental?"

"'The' Consolidated Transcontinental Enterprises? Sure. Who hasn't? That company has its hands in just about everything."

"Well, you may not know there are only two real owners. One lives here out on Long Island in the old money section and the other partner lives in San Francisco."

"No, I didn't know that much."

"Colonel Burr MacFay has been a regular client of mine for several years."

"Lucky break for you."

"Well, it's mostly just boring business filings and such, but yes, this business is the primary reason I decided to leave the firm and start my own practice."

"Well good for you Herbert."

"Now the reason I'm telling you this is-"

"I thought there might be a point to all this."

The office door opened and Miss Jacobs walked in with my coffee. I stood up from my chair and turned to meet her as she walked over.

"Thanks Miss Jacobs. I'm sure it will be as good as always."

"Thank you, Mr. Charles. Please let me know if there is anything else you may need," she said with a smile.

"Oh, I will. I'm sure this will be fine though," I said while slightly raising the cup as a sign of approval as she walked back to the front office.

"So Nick, how's the coffee?"

"Oh, uh, I'll let you know. Where were we?"

"Consolidated Transcontinental."

"Oh yes, that's right."

I was only now aware I was still standing and lowered myself back into the overstuffed throne of a chair.

"Nick, she has a fiancé. Focus."

"Tell her she can trade up. Only kidding, never mind. I'm not exactly the marrying kind anyway."

"Like I said Nick, these men are the bulk of my business so I need to pull out all the stops to help them with this. I'll give you a clue as to how valuable these clients are."

"I think I get the idea."

"I'm not sure you do. They've helped Coolidge get in the White House. And I mean seriously helped. With Al Smith leaving office to

16

run for President, they're organizing for a newcomer to run for governor. His name is Franklin Roosevelt. And yes, he is one of those Roosevelts."

"I see. Wait a minute. Isn't Coolidge a Republican?"

"Yes he is."

"I thought so. Aren't the Roosevelts Democrats though?"

"They are. Don't scratch your head about that. Like some other very wealthy business men, they don't really have any political party loyalty. They back the man they think can help the most."

"Help what the most? Them or the country?"

"You'd have to ask them that. I've heard them say if he's a good governor they'll put him in the White House."

"Alright, I get the picture. These guys carry some weight. Or should I say, have influence?"

"I would say that's putting it mildly. I'll hit the high points on this thing Nick. They want both of us to meet with them and give you the details themselves."

"I'm flattered."

"Well you can thank me then. I recommended you. Mr. Finhaden will be coming from San Francisco by train in a couple of weeks. We'll meet him at Grand Central Terminal when he gets in and we'll travel out to Colonel MacFay's on Long Island together."

"Going out to Long Island? If it's for a meeting that would mean an overnight stay."

"Yes. You'll need to pack for the weekend. It's somewhere between Calverton and Westhampton. I'll let you know the exact dates when they tell me."

With eyebrows furrowed and one slightly raised I said, "Herbert, now you know I'm a little busy with another case or two. I still have an agency and my other clients may think otherwise how I manage my time. And I do have overhead too. Plus I have Wynant going on about his Chicago dentist friend."

Macauley slid open the center desk drawer and pulled out an envelope. "Here is your real retainer. I haven't seen it. It was given to me sealed. You look at that first before turning the job down. If after looking at that and you want out just hand it back and say goodbye. Nick, this could be the window of opportunity for you to branch out. Just think about it. Besides that, when did you really care about Wynant or any of his crazy family? You know they're all nuts. Everyone one of them. Except maybe Dorothy. Strike that. She is too."

I took the envelope as I nodded in agreement. I held and looked at it for moment in silence.

"I never said anything about turning it down but—"

"Well?" he asked.

Without answering I tore it open and looked at the check inside. "This is only the initial retainer?"

"Yes."

"Is this check real?"

"It is."

"I'll be waiting on your call."

"I'll call out to Colonel MacFay's and let him know everything is proceeding. Between his staff and us we'll pull this all together and make a long weekend retreat out of it. And you can rest easy."

"Rest easy? About what?"

"The Colonel keeps a nicely stocked bar."

"A man after my own heart. I guess I'll head out now," I said as I stood and started for the door, "I need to get a few things out of the way before we go."

"Stay close to your phone."

Taking my hat and coat from the tree I turned to Mac. "You know you can usually get me with no more than a couple of calls even while I'm running the streets. I'll be looking for the call and give Carol a heads up on it. She'll get the message to me."

"Good," was all Macauley said as he went back to sorting through the pile of papers on his desk.

3

I made my way from Macauley's office and walked
back to my car. It was only a couple of blocks away
and I actually welcomed the stroll. The spring air
and warm weather had taken far too long to get
here. After a few minutes walking along Coney
Island Avenue I found my ragtop. Turning the key
to bring her to life I was thinking Brooklyn isn't a
bad place but I was nonetheless glad to be heading
back to Manhattan. It was getting late in the day and
I needed to get back to Fifty-Second Street.

      Cruising up Coney Island Avenue, my eye
caught something going down on the sidewalk
ahead. A grubby looking mug ran up to someone's
grandmother and grabbed her purse from behind.
She was no easy target, I tell you. She held on and
tried her best to fight him off, but he jerked the
purse so hard the strap broke and she fell to the
sidewalk. This didn't set too well with me.

      He ran in my direction and made the corner.
I shot through the intersection and drove parallel to
him as he ran along the sidewalk. I sped up a bit and
turned into a mid-block alleyway cutting him off.
He stopped near the passenger side of my car which
was now blocking the sidewalk.

"Move the car, old man," he yelled as he pulled out a switchblade, snapping it open to show me he meant business.

"How about no?" I said as I pointed my Smith & Wesson.

His hand sprung open and his knife went into an end over end spin as it fell to the sidewalk. He quickly spun around and ran the four-forty back to where he started. I backed out of the alley and accelerated in reverse down the street in pursuit. After driving a half a block backwards, I realized I couldn't chase this guy around town all day while driving backwards. I slid the car around as I continued to accelerate. The Stutz BB Boattail never stopped pulling. Shifting from reverse to forward gear in the spin was one butter-smooth motion as it slid into the new gear and continued the pursuit without a hint of a hiccup.

Back at the intersection I pulled a hard left and slid to a stop on the crosswalk. Her handling at the turn was pure poetry. Junior ran smack into the side of the car at a full run and fell back into the crosswalk flat of his back. He couldn't speak or breathe but stared at me with wide 'deer in the headlight' eyes.

"Officer, will you please have someone clean this up? He's blocking traffic," I said to the beat cop as he ran over to us. I opened the door and stepped out.

I relieved the track star of the pocket book. The officer took over the care, custody, and control of his charge as I walked back to grandma. "Ma'am, are you alright?" I asked as I handed her the purse.

"All I can say is, it's a good thing you were driving that car and not me. I would've run over that little dewdropper hoodlum myself!" She glanced over to the cop and thief before turning back to me. "Thank you dear."

"My pleasure ma'am."

I made my way back to the car blocking the crosswalk, and almost made my getaway. With more of New York's finest arriving on the scene, the beat cop came over to me as I got in. "Nick? Nick Charles? Is that you?" he inquired.

"Good afternoon officer. The one and only."

"Well, well… how does that breezer of yours ride when you're not racing down the street backwards?"

"I have to admit driving forward is much better. Especially when it stops the likes of *him* from assaulting little old ladies. Look, I'd love to sit around and kick the can with you fellas but I really have to go iron my shoelaces."

"Oh, alright Nick. Don't take any wooden nickels."

"Thanks, don't worry. You either."

I got the Stutz fired up and was on my way to 42nd Street and Park Avenue. I glanced in my rearview mirror and saw the officers putting our friend in the Paddy Wagon. From the size of the crowd that had gathered, it looked like the boys were actually helping him out. He probably won't snatch handbags in that neighborhood again.

4

Since Mac was coming from Sheepshead Bay and I'm based in Midtown, I drove directly to Grand Central to wait for him there. The plan was to meet at the E 42nd Street entrance. After I finally found a place to park I made my way to the terminal. I saw him already standing outside the doorway, engaged in a conversation with an attractive young lady. "Macauley?"

He turned. "Nick! How are you?"

Shaking his hand, I replied, "Well Herbert, thanks. And you?"

"Nick, this is Letitia Finhaden, Mr. James Finhaden's daughter. She got in from Poughkeepsie late yesterday and spent the night next door at the Commodore."

"I see."

"Just call me Letty," she chimed in as she too extended a hand of greeting.

"Okay, Letty, I will, thank you. I'm Nick."

"I heard."

"So, Poughkeepsie? I thought you lived in San Francisco."

"I do. For now I'm still in school at Vassar. My father scheduled his trip to New York to coincide with our interim break so I could spend some time with him."

"Oh, okay. That worked out nicely for you."

"Yes, it did."

I realized I could talk with Letty for the rest of the day. But I also knew I was there on business and needed to remain professional. I was intrigued by her and thought I might like to know more about her, but today was not the day.

Although she initially came across as a refined and dignified young lady something told me she was really a bearcat of a girl and very capable of holding her own.

"So, you're the big detective I hear. What's the caper you're working on now?" she continued.

"I'm actually between *capers* at the moment. You know how it is for us 'gum-shoes'?"

"Well, when you do you'll have to fill me in. I hear you really know your onions and I do enjoy a good mystery story."

With that invitation I knew we would continue our conversation sometime later.

Macauley chimed in. "Look Nick, Mr. Finhaden phoned my office from Chicago late yesterday. My secretary told me he was scheduled to arrive this afternoon at 4:40 on Track 7. It should be the Illinois Central 134. We probably should start making our way down there."

"I'm right behind you." I turned back to Lettie as I pulled the big brass bar on the door. "Ladies first," as I gestured with my free hand. She ever so slightly dipped her head and walked past me into the building. Macauley made his way in and we were off to the platforms.

The Illinois Central 134 rolled into the station on Track 7 just as Macauley said it would. It always amazed me how they could calculate their exact arrival times. Mr. Finhaden found us before we saw him. Through the jumbled crowd egressing from the train he managed to pick his daughter out. As Mac and Lettie strained to find him in the moving crowd he materialized in front of us from nowhere. "Letty," he said to his daughter as she spun around and threw her arms around his neck.

"Father, how have you been?" she squealed with delight.

"Fine, fine, and you dear? You must tell me how school is going."

Macauley and I stepped away a bit to give them their private reunion and continued our scheming and plotting.

"By the way Nick, I saw where the couple who killed the woman's husband were convicted. That was some good work tying up those little details for the prosecution. I hear they're about to go to sentencing."

"Thanks. Considering how that all went down I'm sure they'll be on their way up to Sing Sing in no time. Sad in a way, her leaving behind a young daughter to be raised by strangers. The whole thing was just so stupid."

"You're right about that. Her husband is dead. Now, I'm sure her boyfriend will be dead and she will be dead. All three gone and the little girl an orphan. And for what?"

"I know."

Letty and her father turned to us. "Father's a bit tired from the long ride. We thought we would go back to the room and let him settle in for a few minutes and then find dinner."

"Let us help with the baggage and get you moved in," I said. "Do you like seafood?"

"Why, yes, very much." Mr. Finhaden nodded.

"May I recommend the Oyster Bar? It's right here in Grand Central but it's no hash house. It's been here since the place opened."

"Thank you, I believe we will. I don't feel much like traveling anymore today."

"You folks wait here. I'll go down to the baggage car and find your luggage. Come on Mac, I may need your help."

"Thank you young man. Look for car 3312. About four from the end."

"Thanks," I answered as Macauley and I started down the platform. Moving further away from the Finhadens, but still wading through a crowd, I asked, "So that man owns half of Consolidated Transcontinental?"

"Yes he does," Macauley answered matter-of-factly.

"And that's his daughter?"

Macauley just cut his eyes at me to answer that one.

"No really? Don't give me that look. My inquiry is purely professional and honorable."

"Yeah, I just bet it is."

"Wait. Here's 3312. It's a baggage car but they haven't slid the door open yet. So where is his wife?"

"Finhaden's wife?"

"No Mac, the guy standing there behind you. Yes, Finhaden's wife."

"He's a widower. He lost his wife during the big flu outbreak in '18. He never remarried and has been raising Letty by himself since."

"I see."

"If you're thinking about trying anything with this girl you better tread very lightly, my friend."

"Now you know I am very capable of keeping my private life and business dealings completely separate."

"And I'm just saying it better stay that way. When this guy was a young buck he really was a cowboy out west riding horseback on cattle drives. Those tough guy cowboys you read about in the dime novels as a kid? Well, he was one in real life."

"Oh yeah, I remember reading the Nick Carter and Secret Service dime novel adventures when I was about ten. So he was one of those guys?"

"He was indeed."

"Thanks. I'll remember that. They're opening the baggage car."

Macauley and I made our way back to the Terminal after getting Mr. Finhaden and his daughter back to their room at the Commodore. "Look Herbert, I'm going back home. I know he's tired and is not driving out to MacFay's tonight.

You can stay and the three of you go over the preliminaries over dinner and then everyone can get a good night's rest. Call me in the morning."

"I guess you're right Nick. I don't even feel like driving up to Colonel MacFay's tonight. I'll just call you at home with the details tomorrow. Just pack and rest up."

I started back to my car. "Good night Mac. In the morning then."

It had been a long day and I was starting to feel it. All I really wanted to do was to find my bed. I found myself driving rather slowly through the city blocks as I navigated my way home through a brain fog. When my apartment building came into view up ahead a tremendous sense of relief came over me. Home at last.

After I parked in front of my place, I sat for a moment of peace and quiet. My head wasn't as clear as it was a short time ago and I wasn't even drinking. Before I could muster up the energy to get out I saw a hack roll past and stop in the street just ahead. The fare got out, paid the driver, and as the cabby pulled away another crate rolled past and stopped in the same place. This time the car pulled to the curb and parked. A woman stepped out from behind the wheel and walked around to the curb. The guy who just paid for a cab ride walked up to her. It looked to me to be one of those clandestine trysts so I was about to get out and go upstairs. But when I saw the pair walking toward my flophouse I decided to stand fast and let them get by.

As they walked past his jacket flapped open in the evening breeze and I could see he was wearing iron. I wasn't paying them much attention before but now I thought I'd watch to see what they were up to. For all I knew, he was a torpedo and the tomato was his stooge. They turned and headed up the walkway to the front door of my building. When I saw him using his index finger to read the mailbox names I began making serious mental notes. I was some distance away, but it looked as if they were paying special attention to my box.

After they looked back and forth at one another conversing about the mailbox, she entered the building and he walked around to the corner and out of sight. I decided it was probably in my best interest to blow and started the car. I wasn't exactly at my best right now and it wouldn't be hard for them to get the bulge on me if they came gunning for me. Slowly pulling from the curb I eased down the street. When I got up to her car, I made note of the license plate

At this time of day there weren't too many options for me to spend the rest of the night. At first, I stopped back in at Studsy's place and killed about an hour there. After my nightcap I went back home, only this time I eased through the alley behind the building. I came back out of the alley on the other end and made two slow passes around the block. I didn't see the car anywhere. When I was finally convinced my visitors had left, I parked the car and started for my apartment. As I inserted my key into the door, Asta began to bark louder than normal. The key seemed to hang up a little, but it finally went in the door knob and I entered. Asta immediately stopped barking when he recognized me.

An uneasy feeling rushed over me. I couldn't put my finger on what the problem was, but I felt I couldn't let my guard down just yet. Asta was acting like his old self now but his greeting when I arrived was highly unusual. I walked throughout the entire apartment conducting a very slow and methodical assessment. Although Asta was acting normal and wanted to play, I still carried my gun room to room.

After some time, I finally came to grips that I had not been burglarized. Everything seemed to be in its place. Then I remembered I had a little trouble getting my key in the door. That had never happened before either. With a flashlight I stepped back into the hallway and examined the keyway much closer than before. I noticed a few new, very shiny, scratches around and going into the keyway. It looked as if someone had tried to enter the door with a different key or possibly someone tried to use lock picks.

When I went back in I went straight back to my personal office and started looking in there again. I finally found what I'd been looking for. Someone had come in while I was gone and they came in for only one reason. My files had been tampered with. Whoever that couple was coming to call on me were looking for a file. Something I'm working on. Nothing was missing so I still don't know what they were interested in. Or who they were.

5

Morning came too early for me. Especially since I was delayed in getting to bed by my late-night visitors. My phone rang. Almost knocking over the candlestick I was finally able to grab it and pull the receiver off the hook. "What?"

It was Macauley asking, "Nick?"

"I think so."

"Are you still asleep?"

"Yes. I am."

"Good, I need to tell you we're planning on leaving out for MacFay's as soon as you can get back over here."

"I'm as good as there."

"Seriously Nick. Don't go back to sleep. We leave in one hour with or without you. Try a bit of the hair of the dog if that's what it takes. Bye."

"Alright, alright. I told you-" the sound of a click interrupted me. I guess he was serious. I clicked the receiver a couple of times and the operator came back on the line. "Operator. How may I direct your call?"

"Would you please connect me to Judson 6-0247?"

"Hold please," came her response and the line seemed to go dead.

Soon Guild's voice was booming over the line. "Lieutenant Guild, Homicide Division."

"Guild, Nick Charles.

"Well Nick. How are you? What can I do for you?"

"Lieutenant, can you to check a license plate for me?"

"Sure Nick. I'll take care of it personally. What is it?"

"It's a Vermont license plate. The number is 62-354. You can leave the information with Carol in the office. But no one else for now, okay?"

"Alright Nick. What's up?"

"I'm not sure right now. I think they were casing my place last night. They might have even been setting up an ambush. Then again, it may be nothing."

"It's just like you to be clear as a bell about things. Rest easy I'll get it for you."

"Thanks. Talk to you later."

After my call with Lieutenant Guild I pulled myself from under the covers and forced myself make my date with Mac. It took a while, or felt like it took a while, but I finally got out of the building and was on my way.

As I turned the corner I could see Macauley's car parked in the front door of the Commodore. They had just closed the trunk and were stepping back onto the sidewalk when I eased up and stopped behind his car. Before I could step out Macauley looked up and waved. Making my

way to them I offered morning salutations.
"Herbert…" I turned to the Finhadens, "Good
morning Mr. Finhaden." I tipped my hat as I turned
to Letty, "Miss Finhaden. Herbert, I'm just going to
follow you in my car. With all four of us going out
there, and for that long, I'm sure your car will be
stretched to the limit on space."

"I guess you're right. It would be a little
cozy but we could make one car work."

"No Mac, I insist. It's no trouble at all."

"If you say so."

"I say so."

Letty added, "Father, would you mind if I
rode with Nick? I mean, it would give you and Mr.
Macauley a chance to talk all that boring business
stuff in private and it would bore me to tears just
sitting in the back all the way out there."

Mr. Finhaden looked at Nick and turned
toward Macauley. "They'll be fine," Herbert told
him. "They'll be right behind us the whole way."

"Alright Letty. I guess it's okay if Mr.
Charles doesn't mind. I don't think he's even been
asked yet."

I said, "Why, it's no trouble at all. It would
be my pleasure to escort Miss Finhaden to Colonel
MacFay's." I extended my arm and said, "Miss
Finhaden?"

"Thank you, Mr. Charles," she replied as she
took hold of my arm.

We continued the exaggerated formalities all
the way back to the side of my car. Mac and Mr.
Finhaden had closed the doors on Mac's car and
were waiting for us. I opened her door and gestured

for her to enter, "Miss Finhaden, your chariot awaits."

"Why, thank you ever so much kind sir."

As we made our way through midtown up Lexington Avenue Letty got right to the interview. "So, you're the great Nick Charles?"

"I don't know about great, but yes, I am Nick Charles. No, wait. Come to think of it, I am a living legend in my own time." I extended my right arm out toward her. "I would ask if you wanted to touch me but you already did." Pulling it back I finished with, "Sorry, only one to a customer."

"And a comedian too. Bonus. Anyway, that's what everyone says. Your detective work has been covered in all the papers. I followed that case last year about the married woman having that affair with the door to door salesman. The one where she got him to help her kill her husband."

"Yes, Macauley and I were talking about that just yesterday. So what are you majoring in up at Vassar?"

"Not so fast. I'll get to that but do tell. What happened with that case?"

"You already know. It was in the papers."

"No, really. I know they don't report everything. They don't know everything. But you do."

"I would like to tell you all about it but I really can't. Not now. You see, this is a capital case where two people are awaiting possible execution. Since things can go in any direction with stays and appeals and such I can't discuss the details. If this ever reaches a final conclusion I will tell you its secrets."

"Alright, I guess. What can you talk about?"

"How about you?"

"Really?"

As we motored across the East River and traversed the Queensboro Bridge with the top down, the warm breeze and blue sky filled the car. Looking down at the flowing water and helter skelter wakes of the watercraft it almost felt, if for only a moment, as if we were flying. If this morning was a sign of things to come, this was going to be a great outing.

"Yes, really," I said. Then came a quiet stern stare. To break the standoff, I decided to go ahead with, "Okay, I'll start. I was born July 29, 1892 in Sycamore Springs, Connecticut to Dr. and Mrs. Harry Charles. I graduated Sycamore Springs High School in 1910 and then moved to New Haven. I graduated from Yale in 1914…"

"Yale!?"

"Yes, Yale. No big deal, really… and then goofed off for a year in Europe. When I got home I tried my hand at medical school but it didn't work out. Come 1916 I joined the NYPD but a year later I was drafted. They told me the Army needed me more than the Police Department because I had been on for just a short time and was a college graduate. I went back to Europe in 1917 as an Army Lieutenant and stayed for the duration of the war. A side note here; I met Herbert Macauley over there when he was assigned to my group. We actually saw a little combat together over there fighting alongside the limeys in Northern France. Anyway, about a month after the war ended I mustered out and shipped back home. Being only twenty-six at the time, the NYPD took me back but I left them again in '21 to work for the Trans-American Detective Agency. I had another Army buddy already working there and he wouldn't let me rest until I came over. By '24 I was able to go solo and I've worked alone since. There you have it. My life story summed up in two minutes. Now you."

"Really? That didn't tell me anything. It sounds like you read a resume. Or an obituary."

"Ouch. That's a little harsh."

"Thank you. I tried."

"I told you everything about me. There's really nothing there. Now tell me a little about you. For instance, tell me about your name. Were you named after anyone? Another family member for example? Letty is not exactly a common name."

"There's nothing wrong with 'Letty'."

"I didn't say there was. I just said it isn't common. A little touchy, aren't we?"

"Well, alright. I was named after both of my grandmothers. Letitia Lenora. Letitia was my father's mother and Lenora was my mother's mother. I say 'was' as if past tense. My maternal grandmother, Lenora is still with us and lives in San Francisco too. Very traditional actually. I am a native of Montana. I was born there in May of 1906. My father was a cattle rancher at the time."

"Well, well, a Montana cowgirl disguised as a Vassar débutante."

"Very funny Mr. Charles. There's that comedian coming out again. Although my father did, in fact, teach me how to ride horses and shoot his guns. I guess maybe you're right after all."

"Letitia Lenora, eh?"

"Yes."

"Seems to me Lenora might be a better fit for you."

"Oh?"

"Yes. Say, what do you think of 'Nora'?" I asked. "Then you won't have to get so defensive again. And it might even make your grandmother smile."

"Nora? Hum."

"Nora. I like that name. It fits you better. You look like a Nora. Nora it is."

"Alright. I'll try it on and see if it fits. Ok Nicky. You may call me Nora."

"Nicky? Now wait a minute-"

"No, you wait. If you can call me whatever you want to, then so can I."

I guess she had me with that one. I could see now she was not going to be the average subservient fawning female. She had a mind of her own and spoke what she thought. I liked that. "So, Nora, tell me more about Montana."

"Not much to tell. It's out west, nothing there, and became a state in 1889. My father spun a shipping business out of his ranching days and we moved to San Francisco when I was still just a little girl. My mother passed away about that time during the big flu epidemic in 1918. I really don't remember much about living in Montana even though my father never sold the ranch. He still owns it but hardly ever goes back. He has employees there who keep it running. I feel like San Francisco is really my home."

"I'm sorry to hear that about your mother."

"Thank you, Nick, but it's alright now. I guess the one good thing that came from it was that my father and I have become very close over the years. We're all we have left. He's concentrated on me and building his businesses. He's never made time for another woman."

"Probably for the best. For you I mean. It must be nice to have such a close relationship with your father. Mine isn't quite as chummy."

"Oh?"

"Oh yes. You see, my father is a physician back home. The problem is that he had big ideas I would also become a doctor and come back and we would work together at his practice. When I dropped out of medical school after the first semester to join the police department in New York he almost disowned me."

"I'm sorry to hear that. It must be very hard to go through life with a strained and distant relationship with a parent."

"You make due. It's okay. Mom's always been supportive of me, but thanks. Say, have you ever been out here to Colonel MacFay's before?"

"Oh my, yes. He's lived out here for years. I've traveled out here with my father since I was a little girl. Colonel MacFay has a daughter a little older than me and we would spend big chunks of our summers playing together. I always thought of her as the sister I never had. Her name is Sandra. We were even roommates at Vassar for one year before she graduated."

"Oh, well you would know far better than I if we're getting close."

"Oh no. I'm sorry but I really have no idea where it is. I never paid attention to landmarks when we would drive out, so I really can't tell. You know, it's a girl thing I guess."

"Macauley told me it's somewhere out on the other end between Calverton and Westhampton. I'm guessing it's just about a seventy-five-mile trip. It could take a couple of hours to get out there."

"That is quite a little car ride" Nora said. "I do remember it always seemed like forever getting out here."

"Yes. So, you're at Vassar?" I replied.

"Yes. I'm majoring in literature with minors in journalism and art."

"Great."

"Yes. I can't decide if I want to teach, write, or draw pictures."

"And you accuse me of being a comedian."

"Who knows what life has in store for us?" she replied.

"I guess you're right. Say, have you had a chance to spend some time back at Grand Central Terminal and take in the artwork there?"

"No, I haven't."

"There's some great stuff there, including the Grand Central School of Art."

"School of Art? At the train station?"

"Yes. It's in the attic space of the east wing. It's a school and gallery. My friend John Sanger works there. If you want I can call him up sometime and arrange for the royal tour."

"Oh yes, Nick. That sounds wonderful. I would love to see it."

As we motored on across the Long Island countryside, the sun rose higher in the sky and the day began to warm a bit. "So has your father told you anything about what's going on?"

"Not really. I think it has something to do with some mobster types trying to extort some money from them. Other than that, I have no idea. My father has always tried to shield me from the tedious details of his business world. This is a wonderful car. What is it?"

"Thanks. It's a new Stutz Black Hawk Boattail Speedster. I've only had it a few months. My friend, Frank Lockley, was able to give me an inside track with the Stutz people in Indianapolis and I special ordered the car with their latest underslung chassis and high performance supercharged engine. They've even sold a slightly modified version of this engine to an aircraft manufacturer."

"I'm sorry, but I'm not really mechanically inclined so a lot of this car lingo will completely fly over my head."

"Gotcha. Suffice it to say the car does everything I want it to. Frank's Indy cars use the same performance upgrades." Little did I know as Nora and I traveled out on Long Island at a leisurely pace, my friend Frank was out at the Bonneville

Salt Flats trying to set a new speed record with a one-of-a-kind Stutz Black Hawk Special.

"How long have we been driving?" asked Nora.

"Oh, about an hour. We should be getting there fairly soon."

"Okay."

"So what do you do for fun? Do you have any special interests? Hobbies?"

"I collect antiques," she replied. "I started my fascination with antiques because of my grandmother. My father's mother. Actually, both of my grandparents on my father's side. They would give me the odd little piece as gifts at Christmas and on birthdays when I was just a child. It stuck with me. I think I still have everything they ever gave me."

"That sounds really nice. A fine hobby and a great story to go with it."

"When I was a kid and we traveled to New York I used to love to go skating at Prospect Park, especially at Christmas time. I haven't gone ice skating in years. I remember going into the skate house to warm up a little when we would stay out so long we nearly froze."

"A regular little Sonja Henie, huh?"

"I'm not so sure about that, but I did have fun. How about you? Did you ever skate?"

"Oh no. Not me. I can't even walk without help much less slide around on those blades."

"I'm sure. You've lived in this part of the country your whole life. You probably taught Gillis Grafstrom how to skate."

"I'm really more of a summer sports enthusiast. Not a big fan of staying outside all day in the winter and freezing my keister off. How about baseball?"

"I like baseball."

"Good. We need to take in a game sometimes. Baseball is the greatest. Specifically, the Yankees are the greatest."

"They're good."

"Good!? Are you crazy? We've got Lou Gehrig and Babe Ruth. You can't get better than that. And we had Hack Wilson over with the Giants up until '25 who hit the longest home run on record that year. He played Left Field when not racking up RBI's. I hate to say it but we lost him to the cubs in '26 and he just keeps getting better every year. Don't make him mad though. He loves to fight."

"You are a fan aren't you?"

"Of course. But the Yankees are the team. Last year they were simply a runaway freight train. Nothing could stand up to them. The main batting lineup was Babe Ruth, Lou Gehrig, Bob Meusel, Tony Lazzeri, Earle Combs, and Mark Koenig. I'm not sure but I think we still have these guys this year. Last July they won a game 21 to 1. That's unheard of."

"That does sound high for a baseball score."

"Yes it is. Not to mention almost shutting out the other team."

"I guess if they're so good they won the championship?"

"I should say they did. They beat out the Pirates to win the World Series. And my money is on them to take home the pennant again this year."

I was finally able to reign myself in on the subject of baseball. I didn't want to over-do it and start boring Nora so I forced myself to hand the conversation back over to her.

"And movies. I do enjoy watching movies. Have you seen the latest Chaplin film?" asked Nora.

"I don't get many opportunities to go out for a movie," I replied.

"Oh, you must see The Circus. It is very funny. But I am a big Charlie Chaplin fan and do so enjoy watching the comedies."

"I guess I prefer comedies to. I did see where a new Marion Davies movie just came out. I think it's called The Patsy. It just came out a few weeks ago and should be playing for some time. Maybe we can work in a day somewhere and try to catch it before they close its run."

"That sounds nice. She is funny too."

We continued to talk about everything under the sun and by the end of the next hour I felt as though I had known her all my life. There was definitely something a little different about this girl I haven't run across before.

"So in a nutshell you pretty much like to test the waters with all types of diversions?" I asked.

"Gather ye rosebuds while ye may," she answered.

"What?"

"Carpe diem," she said, now smiling as if she told an inside joke.

"Oh. Okay. And put very little trust in tomorrow? That's a nice sentiment but you know it's not entirely true."

"You're right. I'm not going to school and learning my father's business to toss it to the wind. I just mean 'seize the day'. Make the most of the moment. But I intend to do so with the future in mind."

"I see."

"I firmly believe every experience we have through life, be it work or play, is a building block of our future self."

"Yes. I see what you mean."

6

It was just before noon when Macauley slowed and turned onto an unpaved road. "Oh! Yes. Now I remember. This is the way to Colonel MacFay's. Things are starting to look familiar. I think we're almost there now," Nora exclaimed.

I turned in behind him and our motorcade continued on. "You know, it just came to me. I think Rosamond Pinchot or some of her relatives live out in this general area too. I remember seeing her in Danton's Death at the Century Theatre back around Christmas," I said.

"A couple of my girlfriends mentioned something to me about that. We were going to come as a group into the city to see it but we never made it. Was it good?"

"Oh yes. A very good performance. At the risk of sounding forward I was going to suggest when another good show is listed I could escort you to a matinée."

"I think I would like that. I'll make sure to keep my social calendar open."

I saw Macauley slowing again. We made another turn and a large estate came into view. Still some distance from the house we were stopped at a large wrought iron gate protecting the roadway. A man stepped out of a small cottage and opened the gate enough to walk through. After a brief meeting with Macauley the man returned to his station and the gate opened fully by remote control. We continued through the entrance and toward the house. I could see the gate closing behind us in the rearview mirror. "Well, I guess business has been good. Look at this place."

"Business has been good. And for quite a long time. Maybe one day we'll need to employ your services in San Francisco and you can visit our house."

"Yes, maybe," I replied as we slowed and came to a stop in front of the mansion entrance. Servants walked out to the cars and began opening doors and asking for luggage. Valets were on standby to park the cars. All we needed to do was get out and walk in. And that's just what we did.

Macauley walked back to me from his car. "Well, Nick, what do think so far?"

"I finally got it.," I said as we walked toward the front steps.

"What?" he asked.

"All this up here on Long Island."

"What about it?"

"Well, this estate, and up here on the far end of Long Island. It all smacks of The Great Gatsby."

"That's a book. This is real. You can put that out of your mind. MacFay isn't young and never throws big crazy parties. This place is more of a peaceful retreat. Almost boring. Oh yeah, MacFay is considered 'Old Money' out here too."

"Good. That's my speed too. But does he keep a bar out here?"

"What do you think? You do know the Volstead Act is not recognized or enforced on Long Island? I thought I told you he did in my office the other day."

"Oh, that's right. You did. Well it looks like things are looking up."

Mr. Finhaden paired up with Nora behind us apparently catching up on the time spent driving out here. As we started up the steps we heard a booming, "Jim! How the hell are you my man? Have a good trip?" Colonel MacFay himself came to the door to greet the approaching assembly.

"Well Burr, it sure is good to see you again. Been a while. It seems to be getting harder and harder to make that cross-country trip anymore," came James Finhaden's reply as we reached the top of the steps and started through the entrance.

"Does anyone need anything? Anyone need a refreshment? Just sing out."

I said, "Refreshment? How about a bourbon and water?"

Colonel MacFay laughed. "I don't know you yet young man, but I already know I like you. I always say never trust a man who doesn't drink. Come this way."

"Well if that's the standard I'm the most trustworthy man you'll ever meet."

After we had a chance to freshen up and get settled in we reconvened in the library. I found my beverage next to an overstuffed oversized chair. There were several others about the room.

"So Nick, Mac tells me you were a major player in that Rose Sanders case last year in the city," said Finhaden.

"Yes sir, that's right."

"What broke the case? I know these things can be drawn out and tedious, but aren't they often solved over a small overlooked detail?"

"You seem to be fairly up to speed on the investigator business. Yes, you're right. They usually are. Especially in cases of murder. The suspect will eventually overlook one small detail in the course of laying out an elaborate ruse. If you can find that little pearl of a mistake you win the contest. Sometimes you stumble across it by plain dumb luck. In this case that's more or less what it was. Dumb luck."

"Do tell."

"Well, you see, Rose Sanders grew to detest her husband. Granted, he did and said things he shouldn't have, but the jury decided they didn't warrant death. Rose should have simply moved out and left him. Instead she crossed paths with a sales rep along the way and started an affair with him. He too was married."

"This thing sounds like a hot mess."

"Oh, it gets better. Harry Graham, the brush salesman, was working Queens when he met Rose. As time went on she came onto him with sob stories of being abused and living a miserable life. The poor sap fell into the trap and kept going back to see her. Once she had him take the bait she enlisted Graham's help to kill her husband."

"And he fell for it?"

"He was a fairly apprehensive at first but eventually gave in. I guess she really put the hocus pocus on him because he was stupid enough to come onboard later. See, she actually tried to kill him on several occasions on her own but failed every time. She came to believe she needed help to get the job done and developed Graham as the recruit."

"Why was she so hell bent to kill him in the first place?"

"Rose started her serious planning when her husband, Allen Sanders, quite openly set out a framed picture of a previous girlfriend and talked openly to Rose about what a wonderful woman she was. You can imagine how this was received."

"He was a very brave man."

"No, he was a very stupid man. And paid the price for it too."

"Yes."

"It seems her first mistake was when she got to thinking it through and a little greed crept in. With the assistance of an insurance agent willing to commit forgery for her, her husband Allen 'signed' a $48,000 double indemnity life insurance policy that paid extra if an unexpected act of violence killed him. Nothing suspicious about that, right?"

"Oh, of course not."

"Then, when Rose felt everything was in place, she and her brush man went in together and overpowered and killed her husband. This was in

March of last year. She later called the police and reported someone broke into their home as they both slept and burglarized the place. She added too much detail and reported having witnessed the brutal murder of her beloved husband and that certain items had been taken. The items she described as stolen actually existed and she had hidden them so officers wouldn't see them while they were in the residence."

"What happened next?"

"Sorry for dragging it out. Believe me, I could go longer with detail, but I won't."

"No, no that's quite alright. Please continue."

"In the following days the ruse began to unravel. First, when Rose was asked to come down and interview with detectives they quickly picked up on her mannerisms and responses. This was not a terrified and panic-stricken wife whom had narrowly escaped death and witnessed the brutal murder of her beloved husband. Not to mention the reported stolen items were located in hiding places within the home during a subsequent search of their residence."

"Oh really? But was that enough to charge her?"

"No. When the police worked the case to what they thought could not be worked any further they knew she was involved but also knew they could never convict in court with what they had. This is when they called me to step in as a consultant. And this will answer the question you posed a little while ago."

"I'm on the edge of my chair."

"The big break came when I found a slip of paper with the letters 'H.G.' on it. It was a keepsake Allen kept from his former lover Harriet Green. When Rose was asked about a note found in the desk with those initials on it she became flustered, almost confused, and asked what Harry Graham had to do with the murder. You see, up until then no one knew anything about this Harry Graham. As it turned out Rose's lover and Allen Snider's old flame, Harriet Green, share the same initials of 'H.G.'. No one knew anything about Harry until Rose panicked and spilled the beans. After Graham was located by the authorities and brought in he sang like a bird."

"You've got to be kidding!?"

"No sir, I'm not. That's what got her."

"Well, well. Interesting."

"Yes. You often have to step back and very slowly see what is not there to get the picture. It's usually a small, seemingly unimportant thing that breaks the case open."

Macauley spoke up with, "You should ask him about the Argo murder. That was a couple of years ago. '25 I think. Or the so-called "Providence" case that originated in Los Angeles. That was an especially gruesome case. I hate talking about what transpired in the commission of the crime, but Nick was especially artful in helping solve the case and bringing the killer to justice."

"Oh?" asked Finhaden.

I spoke up attempting to re-direct the subject to something a little more pleasant. "Well gentlemen, that just happened in December but the defendant, Bill Hillman, was convicted in February. We're still waiting to see how this ends."

The Colonel spoke up asking, "So this Hillman was the man? He's been found guilty and on death row?"

"Yes sir, Colonel. That investigation was extremely comprehensive and there is no doubt he won't be of this world much longer."

"Oh, and I almost forgot about the Ballard and Johnson case from back in '24. Everyone remembers that case," said Macauley.

"You worked that one too?" asked Finhaden.

"Yes sir. That was in the spring of '24 and I was still working for the Trans-American Detective Agency. The Chicago office called on me to travel over there and assist on the case. That was actually thanks to my old friend Jimmy White. He was working in the Chicago office and asked them to send me over there. Jimmy and I pretty much worked that one together. He's still working at that office. The victim, Robert Franklin, was from a wealthy Chicago family who hired our firm to assist with the investigation. Later in the year when the defendants were found guilty, I was in a position to leave Trans-American and start working for myself."

"Well it looks like Macauley's recommendation is not unfounded," said Finhaden.

"Thank you, sir. So I hear you're originally from Montana."

"I'm originally from Missouri but that was way back. I moved out to Montana as a young man after helping other ranchers on cattle drives. The good old cowboy days. Long gone now. Most of my lifelong friends from those days have died out too. Most of 'em were older than me. When I started I was still just a kid."

"Yes sir. That must have been quite a time to live through."

"I enjoyed it and look fondly back from time to time. I guess I should count myself lucky. It was a good life and things seemed to just fall in place developing business ventures from there."

"At the right place at the right time?"

"Yeah, you could say that. Even all the way up to living in San Francisco and running into Burr."

"You mean Colonel MacFay?"

"Yes. Colonel MacFay. Most importantly, to me anyway, was all this time and effort has made it possible for me to provide the very best for my daughter. She's really all I have anymore and means everything to me."

"Yes sir, I understand."

Our conversation tapered off from there and eventually the others joined us. I envied this rare father and daughter relationship. They seemed to truly love one another in the purest of parent child relationships.

"The only thing I really regret through the course of my life was the very first trip I took to San Francisco."

Nora chimed in with, "Father. I've told you about that."

"I know sweetheart, but I can't help it. I guess it'll always haunt me."

"Nick, father has always blamed himself for mother's death and I have told him time and time again he had nothing to do with it. You see, not long after they returned home from San Francisco mother got sick."

"She's right Mr. Finhaden. I know this is probably a sensitive area that is none of my business, but I have to agree with Nora. As bad as that period was you cannot blame yourself. I guess all I'm really saying is listen to your daughter. Not only is she educated and intelligent, but also wise."

"Yes Nick, you're right. She is," he said as his smile returned.

7

The rest of the afternoon and through the evening meal there was no mention of the business at hand. It was almost like a long resort weekend had started with cordial and friendly exchanges and conversations. Then came time for the men to retire to the library. Nora seemed a little frustrated for being excused. Not what one may consider the average young woman. She seemed to have quite an interest in detective methods and how cases are worked. We made our way back across the foyer and reclaimed our seats. Colonel MacFay then addressed us.

"Gentleman. I once again would like to thank all of you for making the time to come out here this week. I thought it would be much more efficient for us all to meet face to face to discuss this and come together on a course of action to deal with it." MacFay gestured toward Finhaden and continued, "Jim here is pretty much up to speed but it seems the problems are isolated to the immediate east coast area. Is that right, Jim?"

"Right Burr. I've received no communications, nor seen any problems in the field or on the west coast. Whatever is starting up and whoever is behind it seems to be focused here."

"Right then. Mr. Macauley and Mr. Charles, I will brief you now and pay the invoices you submit for your consulting fees. Mr. Charles?"

"Yes?" I replied.

"I will go ahead and tell you the reason you are here and under these circumstances is that you come with the highest recommendations from Macauley. As I'm sure you already know, he has been my attorney for quite a long time and I respect his opinions. Welcome to my home, sir."

"Thank you, sir."

"Now I will finally get to the point. At any time anyone needs anything, please feel to move about and get it. This meeting will be very informal and I want everyone to feel at home." The Colonel raised his arm and pointed to the back of the room. "The bar is back there."

I stood from my chair and said, "Well I guess I'll break the ice and start" and started back to the liquor cabinet. The line formed behind me.

"Very good gentlemen. Now our east coast operations staff have been reporting telephone calls, and even in a few cases telegrams delivered, very openly making extortion demands. At first we simply ignored them but recently some employees have quit and management people we need are threatening to resign over being individually threatened with harm, and harm to their families. Finally, a few weeks ago, there was a devastating fire at one of our New Jersey mills. Investigators there have confirmed it was an intentionally set arson. Actually, I believe it was started with an explosion in a nearby parked motor vehicle. Anyway, to make matters worse, I was telephoned directly here at my home by an unknown male voice. He told me if I enlisted law enforcement assistance to investigate, there would be many more. He hinted that he represented a larger organization but, of course, never said who. And if that didn't work, key employees' homes would be targeted. In short, we are being extorted to pay in one form or another."

"This sounds like a very large and well-organized effort. What do you think I may be able to do to help?" I asked.

"We don't know. That's why we asked you to come out here. To run this by you and hear your suggestions. Another reason we chose to have this meeting here is we are well protected and well insulated from prying eyes and ears out here. It appears this problem is close to getting out of hand."

I continued, "But you say there have been no issues, or even hints of a threat, at any other operations and interests in other parts of the country."

"That's right...not yet anyway."

"That is interesting. And you did say someone finally called you direct? Here at this residence?

"Yes. Ideas?"

"Yes. I do have a few. Mainly just generalities at this point. Nothing definite yet but they're forming up. The scope of the suspects' abilities may not be as vast as they would have you believe. In fact, this could, by and large, be a ruse put on by as few as one or two people. I don't know anything yet but this may be a case I can take and solve for you. Let's give it a go."

"Very good. The job is yours. Just let me know if there is anything you need."

"Another bourbon."

MacFay gestured toward Macaulay, "Herbert, get the man another bourbon."

I turned toward Macauley, "Yes Herbert, get the man another bourbon." As I sat waiting for my drink the first thing that came to mind was how anyone knew the private direct phone number to Colonel MacFay at his private Long Island residence. I did confirm with MacFay his number is a private unpublished number that no one has unless specifically given by Colonel MacFay himself. And that is a short list. The prime suspect, or suspects, must be an insider of sorts.

"I would also like to let everyone know my daughter Sandra and her husband Duie should be arriving here sometime tomorrow. They live in Vermont and will be driving in from there," the Colonel added.

The 'meeting' had adjourned and Nora had been permitted to rejoin the gathering. At MacFay's news of his daughter's visit Nora said, "Oh, Sandra's coming? That's wonderful. I haven't seen her since the wedding!"

"Yes dear. I told her on the phone you were coming out with your father. She is looking forward to seeing you again too."

"My, it was before my birthday last year, about the time she graduated, she and Duie came down here for their wedding. It's hard to believe it's been almost a year since I've seen her. I remember her telling me she met him during her last year of school when she went to Europe during the break. I think it was Germany where they met."

"Yes dear," answered Colonel MacFay, "That's where he's from. I guess it's alright, I mean the war has been over for ten years now. It ought to be."

"Oh yes Colonel," replied Nora. "The war ended ages ago. Everyone are friends again and with President Wilson's League of Nations in place now you know there will never be another war like that one. Who am I telling? The Secretary General, Sir Eric, is a friend of yours."

"I suppose you're right Nora. I'm just an overly cautious old man, I guess."

8

The next morning after breakfast I went ahead and started back alone for the city. I pretty much had everything I needed to start looking into things plus I needed to check in with a couple of other clients. I called my office just before leaving MacFay's. My secretary told me Clyde Wynant dropped in to report someone had actually taken a shot at him in front of his house. I told Miss Landers to call him back and schedule a meeting. After the call and loading my suitcase in the car I had a moment with Nora. "I wanted to tell you I enjoyed the company and conversation riding out here yesterday."

"Me too, Nick. Any chance we'll bump into each other again?"

"I think that's a safe bet. You are staying with your father back at the Commodore, right?"

"Yes."

"Alright. Then I'm sure of it. If you're so inclined, call my office when you're back in the city. Maybe we can go out to Chelsea's on the Square for brunch one morning before you have to go back to school."

"That sounds nice. I will."

"Good. Take care of yourself and I'll be seeing you," I said as I opened the car door and got in.

"Be careful, Nick" Nora said in a slow and deliberate manner. The drawn-out tone of voice made me ask, "Careful? Careful of what?"

"Of whatever you're going to get into. I know what you're here for and what you're going to do. Be careful."

As I pulled the door shut and turned the key I said, "I will, Nora. I'm looking forward to our brunch date." The ignition whined briefly, and then the engine purred. Nora walked back around to the walkway and I eased the clutch out.

When I got back to the city I met Clyde at his shop in the 100 block of East 51th Street. When he opened the side door in the alley I asked, right away, "So tell me, what's going on now?"

He stepped outside with me and pulled the door shut behind him. "Well, a couple of days ago I stepped out the door here and started to the corner mailbox." We moved out of the alley entrance onto the sidewalk and he pointed to the corner indicating where the mailbox was.

"A car came up the street from that direction," he said while pointing back in the opposite direction. "As it passed by someone inside started shooting at me. I think it was a tommy gun. It seemed to fire forever. I fell to the ground and tried to get under a parked car. The shooter kept going and turned right up at the corner. I didn't see anyone else around so I know it was Rosewood trying to kill me. I told you he's been threatening to

61

do something. The last time we spoke he said he would blow up my house. This man is crazy!"

"So you didn't see who was in the car?"

"Well, no. But who else could it be?"

"Well Clyde, it could have been Santa Claus for all we know. Look, down here in the Bowery anything can happen. I know you're upset about being shot at but if you can't tell anyone anything more than a car drove by and someone shot a gun, there's not much that can be done. I know what the cops will say."

"Yeah, they said the same thing."

"Did they write it up?"

"No. The beat cop came around and when I told him he just blew it off."

"Look, the Tenth Precinct is just up the street. Go down there and at least have them write up a report. If you need to, tell them I sent you down there. I'm back from Long Island and I'll touch base with my contacts in Chicago and see if they can get a line on this Rosewood fella over there. You did say he told you that's where he's from?"

"Yeah Nick, that's what he said. I even have a telephone number for him. Or at least he said it was his number."

"Were you planning on giving that to me or were you just going to let me figure that out on my own too? Alright, alright, never mind I said that. Give me the number. I know some guys in the Trans-American Chicago office that will run this down for me. Can I call your office and leave word with Tanner or would you rather I tell you direct what we get?"

"Me. Call and speak with me. Don't tell Tanner anything. I'm not completely sure I can trust him or Julia."

"I understand that. I can't really say I blame you. Alright Clyde, keep a low profile and an eye out for anything else and I'll get back with you as soon as I find out anything. Then we'll go from there."

"Okay. Thanks."

"And call the police and Mac and then me if he tries again."

"Okay Nick, I will. I had a report made on that other thing you told me to."

"Good Clyde. Keep it up. I'll catch up with you later."

"Thanks for coming by Nick."

A few more days passed, and everything was business as usual. A couple of other clients had come and gone, and I called Macaulay's office to check in on the Consolidated Transcontinental case. His secretary told me he hadn't returned yet but would forward my message. I began wondering if Miss Finhaden and her father were still out on Long Island too.

I stopped by the Precinct near Wynant's and learned there was no report on the drive-by shooting. While I was there I also took the opportunity to check the tag number from the car that parked at my place the night the Finhadens arrived since I hadn't heard from Guild yet. I'd been so busy I almost forgot about it. The Vermont license plate told me who the mug was who owned the car but I still didn't know who the skirt was I saw driving it. And they were backlit from the street lights so I didn't get a clear look at their faces. Maybe it was just a private audition after all.

There could have been a number of reasons no report for the shooting was found so I walked down to his shop to check it out myself. Since I was there I stopped by to have a quick word with him but there was no answer at the door. After canvassing the area, I couldn't substantiate what Clyde told me. Clyde is an odd bird but why would he tell me this when it didn't happen?

The next morning, I dropped by the office and there was a note on my desk. It seemed Nora and her father got back to the Commodore late in the afternoon the day before and she called. I phoned the hotel and was finally connected to the switchboard.

"Commodore Hotel. How may I direct your call?"

"Yes ma'am. My name is Nick Charles. Could you connect me to Suite 714 please?"

"Hold please."

I heard a click on the line and heard nothing but silence. After a short wait I heard another click and then, "Hello?"

"Nora? Nick."

"Oh Nick, it's good to hear from you. How've you been?"

"Fine. I got your message when I came in this morning and thought I'd see if you're still up for that brunch?"

"I'm actually busy today. Sandra came back to the city with me and she's here today."

"Oh."

"So how about taking me to dinner tonight?"

"Oh, well fine."

"So… where are you taking me?"

"Well, we could cut down on travel time and traffic and go to the Yale Club. It's only a couple of blocks from your hotel and we can take a nice stroll over there."

"That sounds wonderful."

"Or if you prefer we can slip in the backdoor of Chumley's."

"Very funny Nick."

"Oh, so you know Chumley's?"

"I've heard of it."

"I bet you have."

"I've got to go now. Be here at seven."

"Well alright then. See you at seven. Bye."

"Bye Nick."

I hung up the phone and my work day was over. A few hours later I was circling Grand Central looking to park the car. Traffic had eased up a bit and it didn't take long to get parked. I walked through Grand Central Terminal and came out at the main entrance then walked next door. Nora was waiting in the lobby saving me a trip upstairs. I saw her before she saw me. "Nora."

Her head spun around and I saw her magnetic smile. She looked like royalty. "Nick. It's so nice to see you again."

I extended a bent arm. "Shall we go, Madame?"

"Oui mon ami. Laisse nous partir."

"I guess that Vassar education did pay off." She took my arm, still smiling. "Not really. You can pick that up in high school. But it's sweet that you said it."

"I wouldn't know about either one. I got my education reading all of Haldeman's Little Blue Books."

"You probably know more than most if you did. But I must say, I've already caught you in a lie."

"Oh?"

"Yes. Don't you remember in the car going out to Colonel MacFay's?"

"I'm not sure."

"You rattled off a dry sounding rundown of your autobiography but I listened. You told me you graduated from Yale University in 1914."

"Oh, I did, didn't I?'

"Yes, you did. You do know Vassar is Yale's sister college?"

"Indeed, I do. That makes us practically relatives."

We continued walking up the Vanderbilt Avenue side of Grand Central Terminal. The Yale Club was only a couple of blocks up between 44th and 45th Streets. When we crossed the street at 43rd Nora said, "Is that Sandra?"

"What?" I said.

"Sandra. I think that's Sandra walking toward us." Nora shouted ahead as she waved one hand in the air, "Sandra! Here. It's Nora." The woman in question stopped and focused on where the voice came from.

"Well, Nora. What a surprise running into you out here" replied Nora's friend Sandra as we all converged along the walkway.

"What are you doing here? I thought you went home today?" asked Nora.

"Well, we were going to but decided at the last minute to take in one more night in the city. You know, just one night of me and Duie alone for a night out. It's been such a busy week and we always seem to be in a crowd."

"I must admit I know the feeling. Oh, where are my manors? You remember Nick, don't you?" Nora said as she re-introduced us.

Extending her hand she replied, "Oh yes, how are you tonight Mr. Charles?"

"Very well Mrs. Schlusser, thank you. It is Schlusser, right?"

"Why yes Mr. Charles, it is. Thank you for remembering."

"So, Mrs. Schlusser, where is Mr. Schlusser? I assume he is nearby."

"Oh, of course he is. He is parking the car and told me to go ahead."

"Really? Even Manhattan isn't a place you normally see an unescorted lady walking along the sidewalk in the evening. I mean, there is still a certain criminal element about that may be lured out. In short, it's not safe."

"Oh, it'll be fine. I'm just walking to the restaurant inside Grand Central Terminal. Duie thought it was late enough we may have trouble getting a table. So I went ahead while he tried to park and would catch up with me. I do appreciate your concern and advice but I'm practically there."

"Yes. I'll tell you what. Nora and I are walking up to the Yale Club" I said as I turned and pointed up the street "right up there. We'll just loiter here on the sidewalk a bit until you get over there and walk inside. I'll feel better knowing you're not out here alone in the evening."

"Me too" said Nora.

"Well, alright. Thank you so much, both of you, for worrying about me. You two enjoy your evening out too. I'll see you later Nora. Good night." Sandra rattled off rather quickly as she began walking away while still speaking.

Nora turned to me and said, "I thought she left this afternoon heading back home. Sandra and I practically grew up together and were roommates at Vassar until she graduated last year. She's a year ahead of me. But we're practically sisters more than just friends. Sometimes I find myself missing the days we hung out together and would get in trouble. Fun times."

"Oh, I see. A pair of troublemakers, eh?" We entered the building. "I hope you like nice views. We're going to the Roof Dining Room. The Terrace is nice. I think you will like it."

"I'm sure I will."

The evening was perfect. Good drinks, good food, and a dinner companion beyond comparison. Refined, looks, and most important, bright and intelligent. I realized I was starting to like Nora too much. I had no designs on settling down with one woman. I am too busy and too mobile with my chosen vocation. Then again, I am getting a little older and may need to re-evaluate things. Then again, age could be a big deterrent. She's only twenty-two and about to graduate college. I'm 35. I'm not an old man but that's quite an age gap. I could go on round and round like this all night. For now I needed to just put all of this out of mind. Focus on the here and now. "Do you have a preference of entrées? Beef, poultry, or fish? Or are you a vegetarian? Whichever you prefer you'll find something here you'll like."

"I could tell that right away."

The waiter stepped up to the table as soon as we were seated. "Garçon, could you bring the beverage menu? And we'll start with the pickled oyster hor d'oeuvres," I requested.

"Very good, Mr. Charles," he replied as he quickly turned and walked away.

Nora ordered the Cioppino and I stayed with the King Salmon. At least I know neither of us are allergic to seafood. We had one thing in common.

"So I guess you could call this a first date," I said.

"Or dinner."

"Right. That's what it is. Look, if this place is too stuffy for you I know plenty of dives we can hit."

"Well, to be honest with you, I get my fill of this stuff when I'm with father. I love it; don't get me wrong. But when I'm off alone I tend to break it up with a little clean sneak."

"Alright, let's fly and hit a couple of gin mills then."

"Okay, but I'm going to eat first. I never could drink on an empty stomach."

"You sound like you're an old pro at this. How old did you say you were?"

"You should know well and good you grow up pretty fast on the mean streets and at Ivy League schools."

"That's right. What was I thinking? So I guess it's safe to say with your rite of passage you've mastered the ability to put down a few?"

"Now that all depends."

"On what?"

"Where I am. Who I am with. What it is I'm drinking."

"You're not making this easy on me, are you?"

"No."

"Okay. Let's start with the 'where'. What kind of place is conducive for your acceptance?"

"You'll have to take me there first and then I'll tell you."

"Right. I know the perfect place then. Ever hear of the Pigiron Club?"

"I don't think so."

"Alright young lady. Your real education of New York City begins tonight."

"Oh? My real education?"

"Yep. The guy running the place is a chap by the name of Studsy. Studsy Burke. He's a regular Joe and has always been on the level with me. He was pinched for safe breaking but since getting out of stir he's been a straight up kinda' guy. Except of course for running a joint and that doesn't bother me. I'm a patron. And even though it's a little on the lower end of the scale he doesn't allow any quiffs to hang around either. Even Studsy has his standards."

"Well I'm up for it but like I said, we'll have our dinner first. This is too nice to run out on."

A couple of hours later Nora and I found our way to Studsy's. Business was booming tonight. The juice joint was running wide open. I thought we would have to take a number just to get in. When we did get inside we fought our way to the bar. I saw Studsy standing behind the bar at the other end bent over working on something. He looked a little disheveled but that was his normal state. When he saw us he walked down to greet us. "Good to see ya' Nick. You couldn't've timed it better. The music is about to start up again and it's still happy hour." He was right. The band was milling around on the stage.

"Hey Studsy. Is that Franklin Henderson?"

Studsy glanced at the band and then looked back, "Oh yeah Nick. That's Shack."

"The last time I saw him play was at the Club Alabam over on 44th Street."

"He left there a long time ago. Since that joint was legit I think Prohibition killed it. His band records and plays everywhere now. He's only here for tonight and then they're off again. You can see the crowd he drew."

Since the band was just starting to gather it was going to take several minutes for them to get started again.

"Nicky, do you have a nickel?" asked Nora.

"Uh, yeah. Why?"

"Give it to me."

"Okay," I said as I dug into my pocket. "Here."

"It's too quiet in here," she said as she spun around and made her way over to the Audiophone machine. I watched her study its contents, drop the nickel in the slot, and then I heard 'Let's Misbehave' start playing. She turned back around from the machine and smiled a mischievous smile at me. I was intrigued and timorous all at the same time. I turned back to Studsy and said, "That is good news. How long does happy hour last around here?"

"Well Nick, for you it's happy hour in here all the time. So who's the dame?"

"This is my friend Nora. She asked me to bring her here. You should feel flattered."

"Oh you're all wet Nick."

"No Studsy, she did."

"Well, well. What'a'ya know. Just for that the first round is on me sweetie." He said to her as she walked back over to us.

"How kind of you Mr. Studsy," said Nora as she stepped up from her trip to the music machine.

"Think nothin' of it darlin'. It's my pleasure," he replied as he turned away to make the drinks. Nora turned to me with a half puzzled look on her face. She just thought she had been to some

72

places in New York and walked on the wild side. She was about to see different slant tonight.

"That's Studsy. Swell guy really. I sent him up a couple of years ago for larceny but he's over all that now."

"What? And you come here?"

"Why not?"

"Oh Nicky, you do know the nicest people don't you?"

"My dear, you have arrived. It looks like the band is about to reconvene. Would you care to dance?"

"Only if it's a slow one."

"Well, alright." I said just as they opened with Henry Burr's Are You Lonesome Tonight? "I guess we'll dance."

"I guess we will" Nora said as she stepped up to me with her arms out.

As the evening started to turn into morning I suggested I escort her back to the hotel. "I've enjoyed the evening very much Nora but do you think it might be time to call it a day?"

"You're probably right Nicky. Me too. I've had a great time and hate to see it end but it is getting late. Or early. However you look at it."

"May I see you home?"

"Please, sir. Thank you."

We made our way back along the route we walked to the restaurant. As we walked and talked I took her by the hand. She never missed a beat while talking and closed her grip on mine. It seemed as if we had known one another forever.

9

We arrived back at the Commodore after our leisurely walk and it was time to say goodnight. As we entered the grand lobby I said, "Well, I guess this is where the train stops."

"Oh Nicky, you must see me to my door."

"Are you sure that's a good idea?"

"Nicky, you must."

"Well, I guess there's no harm in that. Your father is in the apartment, right?"

"Yes, he is. Now walk me to my door."

We waited for a car, but only for a minute. The operator opened the door and we stepped aboard. No one else was nearby so he closed the door rather quickly and the three of us awkwardly began our ascent. No one spoke other than Nora telling him what floor to stop on.

"Seven please."

"Yes ma'am."

Another minute of silence passed until the car stopped. When he opened the door and we walked past him, he said, "Have a pleasant evening folks." He seemed to be smirking a bit as I glared at

him. Nora and I proceeded down the hall as we
could hear the elevator door closing behind us.

"Friendly chap, isn't he?"

"Oh, never mind that. He'll be alright."

We finally stopped in front of Suite 714 and
Nora removed a key from her handbag. She turned
it in the lock and opened the door. With the door
barely open she turned around to me.

"Nicky, it was a lovely evening. Thank you
so much."

I took her by the hand again and slightly
raising it, I kissed the back of it. "Thank you Nora,
for the wonderful company and conversation
tonight." She gently pulled her hand out of my
grasp and then threw both arms around my neck and
kissed me.

When she let me up for air I called out,
"Nora!?"

"What?" After a brief pause and my wearing
a bewildered look on my face she said, "You have
been nothing but the perfect gentleman. I want you
to know I am very appreciative of that. I also
wanted to let you know I won't break. Now you
may go home."

She turned back to the door and pushed on
into the darkness and I started back toward the
elevators. Just as I was about to press the call button
I heard a muffled scream. The way the building is
so solidly built it was hard to pinpoint. I heard it
again. It was Nora from inside her apartment. I ran
back and barely slowed when entering.
Subconsciously I had drawn my revolver and was
standing in the front parlor looking at her framed in

an open bedroom doorway with it in my hand. "He's been shot," she managed to get out while still crying.

"Are you alright!?"

"He's in there. He looks dead," she continued.

"Nora! Are you okay?"

"Yes, I guess," she continued while sobbing.

"Look, I need you to do this. Okay Nora? I need you to call Guild." I retrieved the slip of paper from my wallet with his home telephone number on it and gave it to her. "Call Lieutenant Guild and tell him you're calling for me. Okay?"

"Alright Nick."

"I'm going to go through the rest of the apartment and check it out while you tell him what happened."

"Okay."

Now conscious I was gripping a revolver, I started making my way through the apartment. I could barely hear the muffled voice of Nora as she spoke on the phone out near the front door. When I returned she was still holding the receiver to her ear. I put out my hand out and she handed the phone to me. "Lieutenant? Are you still there?"

"Yeah Nick. What's going on? I could hardly make out what she's trying to say. I stayed on the line because she said you were there."

"Yes. And thank you. It's Nora Finhaden's father. You better hurry on over with some of your boys and meet us at the Commodore next door to Grand Central Terminal. We're in 714. He's been shot.

76

"I'm on my way Nick. I'm going to call and get some of the fellas headed that way now. It might take me a little longer."

"We'll be waiting."

I hung up the phone and tried to get Nora to sit down. That wasn't going to happen. "Nora, please sit down and tell me what happened. What did you do when you came in?" This, more or less, went on until the first officers showed up from the nearby beat. Fortunately, this wasn't but a few minutes. "Hey Nick! What's up?" asked the first.

"It's Nora's father. He's in the bedroom. I just got off the phone with Guild. He'll be along soon. I guess you guys should just keep the scene safe until he gets here."

The second officer got off the elevator and headed toward us. "Well, Nick Charles. What's going on Nick?"

"Look Pat, I just told Jimmy here what we have. I'm going downstairs with Nora and we'll wait for the Lieutenant there. He should be here soon; I just spoke with him on the phone." I escorted Nora to the coffee shop downstairs, just off the lobby. After we got off the elevator and away from the operator Nora asked, "Nicky, I don't get it. Why? Why would he do this? It doesn't make sense."

"Look Nora, we don't really know what happened yet. The police will go over the room and investigate to the fullest. Things aren't always what they seem. Tell me what you remember doing and seeing after I left you at the door."

"Well, it was dark inside. I walked to the nearest light switch in the hallway near the door. After I turned on the light I could see father's bedroom door was slightly open and his bedside lamp was on. So I thought I would open the door a little and look in on him and say goodnight if he were still up reading. Then as I quietly pushed the..."

"Nick!" said Guild as he approached our table.

"Lieutenant," I said as I stood to meet him. "So, have you been upstairs yet?"

"No. I came in the building through the side entrance and saw you sitting here through the lobby window. So what's going on?"

"Have you met Nora Finhaden?" I asked as I gestured toward Nora as she remained seated.

"How do you do?" he asked as he tipped his hat toward her.

"Look, Lieutenant, she just walked into her apartment upstairs and found her father. He's been shot."

"Oh?"

"She and I have been together all evening and I walked her home from around the corner. We had dinner at the Yale Club. Kelly and O'Reilly showed up after I phoned you. They're upstairs with him now. When the apartment was secure with those two I brought Nora down here for a little peace and quiet."

"I guess I should head on up and see for myself. Just wait here and I'll be back down."

"We've got nowhere else to be. See you on the return trip." As Lieutenant Guild went out the café door I said, "Now Nora, I have to be honest with you, it looked like a suicide. I know that must be unbelievably hard to see."

"Why? I don't understand. He seemed so... so, normal. I mean, I never heard him say anything that would hint at this. He was happy and looking forward to my birthday and graduation and, well, everything. There was no reason for this!"

I really did not know what to say at this moment. Sometimes there isn't anything to say. "Nora, I just want you to know I'm here for you. I know they'll check everything they can and I'll look at it behind them, okay?"

"Thank you, Nick."

The counter girl called over to me from near the register, "Mr. Charles?" As she held up the telephone receiver she said, "Phone."

I looked at Nora as I rose from my seat. "It must be Guild." I walked over and took the phone and answered, "Hello."

"Nick?"

"Yes."

"Nick, I need you to come back up here. I need to show you something."

"I'm on my way." I laid the phone down and walked back to our table.

"The lieutenant?" asked Nora.

"Yes. He wants me to come back up. Just wait here, I'll be right back?"

"Alright Nicky. I'll be right here."

When the elevator opened and I stepped on, I recognized the operator. He was the same guy working it when we went up earlier. "Excuse me sir, but earlier this evening before me and the young lady came in do you remember seeing another couple getting off on Seven?"

"Another couple? No, can't say I have."

"When did you come on tonight?"

"About ten. I do remember a young lady go up there around one or two. She was quite the looker and well dressed. Since it was that time of the day and she was alone and looked so well-heeled I just thought she might be one of those, well, ladies you know."

"Yes. I think I do know. Tell me, did she say anything while riding up? I mean anything at all? It's not important what it was."

"No mister. The ride up was dead quiet. All you could hear was the elevator. Oh, wait. I do remember one thing I thought was a little out of place."

"Do tell."

"Well, like I said, she was definitely no chunk of lead but was wearing cheaters. Imagine that."

"Yes. Imagine that."

Back upstairs Guild wanted to first show me the scene in the bedroom. I had already looked it over, albeit quickly, but his boys had been able to comb through it much slower and more thoroughly. Lieutenant Guild started with, "Now I know this looks like a suicide when you first walk in here, but we may have a problem with this one."

"Oh? A problem?"

"Yeah. For starters we haven't found a note."

"There are some that don't leave a note."

"Right Charles. I know that alone is not decisive, but it does raise a flag in a case like this."

"I agree Lieutenant. Go ahead."

"You see how he's lying flat of his back in the bed and his right arm has extended out away from the body and beyond the side of the bed?"

"Yes."

"Well his revolver was lying on the floor directly beneath his hand. It looks as if he used the gun and when his arm fell away from the side of his head out to his right side he dropped the gun from his hand to the floor."

"And?"

"Well, the gun is a Smith & Wesson K-frame M & P revolver chambered in .38 Special. When I opened the cylinder to check it I found it was loaded with five rounds of unfired .38 Special and the chamber under the hammer had an empty unfired brass casing in it..."

"And? What's the big news here Guild? Of course, the round under the hammer would be an empty case."

"The empty case was a .32-20. Not a .38 Special."

"What?"

"That's right. The spent round was a .32-20. It fits in the chamber and the cylinder will close. I wondered about actually doing that though. It seems to me if you stuck a .32-20 in a .38 cylinder and actually fired it, the brass casing would, at the least, split open from the unsupported high pressure."

"It could. I guess it would depend on how the round was loaded. It could even blow the gun apart if the case had been loaded for a rifle."

"Right. But there are no signs of swelling or splitting. In fact, I can't really tell right now if the gun was even fired. But it had'to'ave since the bullet is in his head."

"Or some bullet is in his head. Do we really know the caliber or origin of the round in the body?"

"Good question, Nick. Actually no, not until Doc takes him away and checks it out."

"And look at the entry wound. That is not a contact shot. That wound was made by a shot fired from a much farther distance."

Guild leaned down and got a closer look at the side of Finhaden's head. "Oh yeah, I think you're right."

"Right. And about mixing in the wrong ammo, there are people who have loaded the wrong ammo in their guns. It's actually not that unusual. If they can make it fit they'll fire it. I guess they don't know any better. Most are lucky that they don't blow their gun up. Sometimes they do. The bullet that Doc shows us will probably be a .32 but I'll put my speculations on hold until we hear from him."

"Good idea."

"Well, Lieutenant, I'm going to go ahead and take Nora back out to Colonel MacFay's. He was Nora's father's business partner and lives up there. We were all out there just a few days ago."

"Alright Nick. I'll call you if I need to talk to either of you later. We'll be busy here for a while anyway."

"Thanks Lieutenant. I'll be talking with you later," I replied as I walked back over to the desk. I took pen and paper and started jotting. "Here Lieutenant, this is MacFay's telephone number if you need us. You can also get word to me there through my office."

"Right Nick. Thanks."

I went back downstairs and sat back at the booth Nora had been waiting in. Nora watched my every move until I settled into my seat and as I raised my coffee cup she said, "Well?"

"Well nothing. He showed me a couple of things but they are inconclusive. We won't know anything until Doc does his thing. And the lab checks the gun over. Right now we're going to finish our cup of coffee and then get you back out to MacFay's."

We finished a second cup of fresh hot coffee and mulled over the possibilities of what happened upstairs. I was beginning to get a few ideas I was keeping under my hat. After a short while and some small talk we made our way back upstairs together so Nora could gather some things she would need out on Long Island.

I met back up with Guild and his crew at the scene as Nora went to her bedroom. After a while I walked over to her room and tapped on the partially open door and looked in. "Nora?"

She looked up quickly, as if I startled her. "Yes Nick?"

"I just finished speaking with Guild. We're not going to know much more than we already do until the autopsy. I told him I would be taking you back out to MacFay's. Get together some things you'll need for a while and we'll go ahead and leave this morning."

"Oh, thank you Nick. I don't know what I'd do without you looking out for me right now. I just can't think straight about anything right now."

"It's quite alright. Now pack for a stay out there and I'll wait back out here."

I left Nora, pulling her door shut, and walked back to Mr. Finhaden's room. The first officer to arrive was still standing near the bedroom door. "Hi Kelly. How've you been doing?"

"Oh, same old stuff Nick. You know how it is."

"Yeah, I guess. I see most of the evidence has already been removed."

"Yeah, the lieutenant took the gun himself. I heard him say something about walking this one through himself. He's not going to let this get bogged down or let anything fall through the cracks. He's a pretty good guy for a supervisor."

"Yes, he is. I'll have to thank him when I see him again. Oh yeah, make sure someone talks to these elevator operators too. Especially the guy working car two. He seemed to be pretty alert and observant for someone working a dead hotel lobby on a graveyard shift."

"Right. Thanks for the tip."

By now the sun had risen and lit up the room. I had an overall sense the room even looked different, so I examined the scene again and even slower than before. As I was finishing my second go at it I started to leave and then there it was. I noticed a slightly darker spot on the frame of the bedroom door. It was about three feet from the floor. This one small dirty spot at the door seemed very unusual especially in that location and in this five-star hotel. I ignored it for the moment and walked back to Nora's room.

"Nora."

"Yes Nick."

"I just wanted to let you know we are in no hurry at all. Please take your time and make sure you don't leave anything behind you may need out there."

"Thank you, Nick. You are sweet."

"Think nothing of it."

Between the excitement and confusion of everything going on and the hustle and bustle of cops and the coroner's crew, along with my new guardian role taking care of Nora, I temporarily lost sight of what I needed to do there. I had become focused on Nora and what she needed and wasn't thinking as an investigator.

"Okay Nora, let's go ahead and get out of everyone's way. Are you ready?"

"Okay Nick, let's go."

I picked up her bags and we started for the door. "Lieutenant, we're leaving now. You have Colonel MacFay's number if you need me."

"Right Nick. See you later."

When we made it back to the elevators and the door opened I didn't recognize the operator this time. "Excuse me, but were you working last night? I mean a few hours ago. The graveyard shift."

"Mister, I've been here all night. Why?"

"You know what's going on upstairs, right?"

"Oh yeah. The whole building knows."

"Do you remember seeing a couple get off on Seven sometime during the night?"

"I remember a few through the night but those folks live here. I know who they are and where they live."

"No one new? Any strangers you don't see regularly?"

"I did see one gentleman get off on Seven alone around one this morning. I didn't notice anything odd about him. I just thought he was a hotel guest."

"You're sure it was around one and he got off on Seven?"

"Oh yeah. I'm pretty good at remembering stuff like that. Oh now I remember."

"Remember what?"

"It was just a few minutes later; long enough to go down and back up, that I saw the guy standing at the same door as when I left him. I still thought nothing of it at the time and went about my business."

"Who were the people you took up after him?

"That's the Pattersons in 722."

"Thank you my good man. It's almost time you can get out of here and go home isn't it?"

"You bet, and I can hardly wait."

The elevator stopped at the ground floor and Nora and I exited and walked across the lobby to the main entrance. It was morning now and the streets were filled with traffic. As we stepped out onto the sidewalk the pedestrian traffic was fairly heavy as well.

"Nora, I have to make a quick stop at my place before we head out."

"Oh?"

"I just need to run up and grab an overnight bag. It's already packed with what I need and I should only be a minute. You can wait for me in the car."

"Oh. Alright Nicky."

We made it to the car and we headed up the street back to my apartment building. In a few minutes I was parking in the door. "Okay Nora just sit tight and I'll be right back." She nodded as I closed the door and headed toward the lobby. Once upstairs I quickly assessed the area, grabbed my overnight bag, and was on my way back downstairs.

Returning to the street and throwing the bag in the back I got back under the wheel and put the car in gear. As we pulled away from the curb Nora stirred awake but quickly dropped back off. After all, we had been up all day and all night before. I was a bit tired myself but was running full steam ahead on caffeine and adrenaline. My priority now was to take care of Nora and see to her needs. And right now she needed to be out at Colonel MacFay's house.

10

We were finally on our way moving at a much better pace on the open road. I told Nora I had already called Colonel MacFay and filled him in on what had happened. Before I could ask to come out he offered his home to her. I told him he did not need to dispatch a car for her as she and her belongings were already loaded into mine and I would be bringing her.

Once outside the city and away from heavy traffic I asked, "So Nora?"

"Yes Nick?"

"Can you tell me anything about what's been going on with your father that may even remotely be connected with this?"

"I've been thinking about that all morning. I still have no idea."

"What can you tell me about his gun?"

"Nothing really. I think it's one he just bought a few months ago."

"A few months ago? You mean it's new?"

"Yes. He ordered it in February, I think, and it came out to him in March. Maybe early April.

Yes, it's brand new. I remember he was so proud when he opened it of the shiny chrome finish."

"So he hadn't had time to become familiar with it?"

"Well, I guess not. But father has had guns his whole life. And he already owns dozens. I didn't know why he kept buying more all the time. But, you know, he was a cowboy. I mean really. He worked our ranch back in the day of real cowboys. That new revolver was nothing new to him."

"Yeah, I guess you're right. I was lucky enough to have one good conversation with him and he spoke of the days he was on cattle drives. Your father was quite a guy. I only wish I could have gotten to know him better."

"Oh yes, that's would have been nice. I heard all kind of stories when I was a little girl. He certainly could spin a yarn. When I was growing up he was bigger than life. I thought he could do anything."

"Do you recall anything going on his life that would have indicated he might do anything like this?"

"No! Not at all. It just doesn't make any sense he would do this. I can't believe he shot himself. I just can't. You saw him when he got here. You've had a chance to talk with him. Did you see anything like this coming?"

"Well my time with him was very short but no Nora, I can't say I did."

We continued on our journey. For a while we rumbled down the road in silence. I was kicking so many things around in my head that just weren't adding up. First, a suicide that caught everyone, and I mean everyone, by complete surprise. No one picked up on any kind of sign and there was no note left. Nothing about anything leading up to it was typical. Then there was the new revolver he carried while traveling. Although it was new, it wasn't new to him. At least there wasn't anything new to him about how to operate it. So, an amateur accident is pretty much out of the question. One doesn't usually carry different caliber ammunition with them on journeys if they're carrying only one gun. It would have been loaded before leaving home and forgotten about unless it was needed. If you bring extra ammunition it would be for that gun. For a man like Mr. Finhaden it was a foregone conclusion he would never make the amateur mistake of loading a revolver with the incorrect ammo.

"Does your father own a .32-20 caliber?" I asked.

"A .32-20? Why do you ask?"

"Oh nothing. I just used to have one myself and it was a fun plinker."

"Oh yes. I think he owns every kind of gun you can buy. He took me with him out to target practice all the time. I know he had .32-20s and .44-40s in revolvers and rifles. I always thought it was neat you could shoot the same ammunition in a handgun and long gun."

The conversation went on from there until we arrived.

"…and then in June I'll graduate," Nora finished.

"That's wonderful. Any career plans for after graduation?"

"I was just going to work for my father. There would be plenty to do."

"I bet there would be."

When we arrived at MacFay's estate, the man at the gate knew we were coming and remembered my car. He opened the gate for us as we approached. I stopped the car at the front door and MacFay met us outside. Nora's side was nearest the house and he greeted her first as she stepped out. "Nora, dear Nora, how are you?" he asked her.

She started crying again and threw her arms around him. She looked like a young heartbroken child. "Oh it was horrible! I don't know why he would have done this!" she barely got out through the sobbing.

I quietly got out and communicated with MacFay's valet about the parking and luggage. "Don't worry about a thing Charles," said MacFay from the other side of the car. "They'll take care of everything. Even the luggage. You both will stay, at least for tonight, and they already know which room to put the bags. Let's go in." I walked around the car and we ascended the front steps.

"Colonel? May I borrow your phone? I need to call my office and let them know I'm here."

"By all means young man. You may use it whenever you need." He pointed toward the library as we entered the foyer. "It's right in there on the desk. Help yourself."

"Thank you." I turned for the library as they continued toward the kitchen. Once behind the desk

I went ahead and took the liberty of sitting in the chair. My first call was to Guild. "Hello Lieutenant? Nick Charles. I'm out on Long Island at MacFay's. Have we learned anything more?"

"No. Not yet, but I can give you Doc's direct number if you like."

"Great. Please. Hold on a minute while I find something to write on." I looked for a slip of paper across the desk top but it was kept too neat. Nothing out of place there so I started pulling open drawers. I spied a Colt Police Positive Special revolver lying in the first drawer. Without picking it up I could see marked on the barrel it was chambered for .32-20. Remembering the Colonel and Finhaden were business partners the thought arose if anything nefarious was afoot concerning any business dealings MacFay could be considered a suspect.

"Uh...look Guild...let me call you back. Better yet, phone my office there in Manhattan and give Carol the number. Something just came up here I need to tend to. Thanks. Bye."

I thought about taking a chance on it not being missed and pocketing the gun. I only needed to borrow it for a short time to get what I needed to answer the question. Then I decided on a different tactic. If I did take it without his knowledge and he found out it could create irreparable damage to our relationship that could last a lifetime. If he is innocent that situation would be totally unacceptable.

"Nick?"

I was slightly startled at the sight of Nora standing in the doorway. "What!? I mean, what?"

"Are you okay?"

"Oh yes. Sorry. My mind was off somewhere else and you surprised me."

"I know that feeling. I was going to ask you if you'd like a cup of coffee."

"I'd love it." I stood and walked to the door. "Please show me the way."

Nora and I walked back to the kitchen as Colonel MacFay met us in the foyer. "When you get your coffee we'll reconvene back in the library," he said to us.

"Right. We'll be right there," I replied. "Say Nora? I know this may not be the best time to ask this."

"Ask what?"

"Well, when I was on the phone a little while ago I needed a slip of paper and pencil. Lieutenant Guild was giving me a phone number. Anyway, I opened a drawer and saw a Colt revolver lying in it."

"And?" she slowly replied with a cynical inflection.

"Well, I thought about asking the Colonel to borrow it for a little recreational shooting while we're way out here in the country. I rarely get to do that anymore."

"Oh. Okay. I see."

"And I was going to invite you along. If you wanted to. I know you've been around guns your whole life and thought you may want to do some plinking too. I guess the stories you were telling me about going shooting with your father put the idea in my head. Are you game?"

"You know, it has been a long time since I was able to get out away from everything and do a little target shooting. Now that you mention it, it may be a good stress reducer and help get my mind off everything right now. I'll ask him."

Once back in the study the three of us tried to dissect what had happened to Mr. Finhaden. Thinking MacFay could be a suspect I strained to appear relaxed and open when all the while I remained guarded in what I said. To my advantage, neither of them knew about the odd ball .32-20 casing found in Finhaden's gun. That is, unless they knew how it got there.

"Nora, did I tell you about Sandra staying on a little longer after you left?" asked MacFay.

"No."

"It's no wonder with everything else going on right now. Anyway, she and Duie came back through from the city and I thought they went home. But a couple of days later they showed up again."

"Really?"

"Needless to say, I was quite surprised."

"I guess."

"They told me instead of going directly home they went to the beaches for a day or two and since they were still close by they would drop in one more time before heading home."

"That was nice of them to think about seeing you again before heading back up."

"Yes it was. It was good to see her again so soon. Lately it has been long stretches between visits. I understand we do get busier as we become adults, but I still don't like it."

"Does she know?" asked Nora.

"About your father? No. I don't think so. I haven't had the time to call her yet. Besides we really don't know what happened yet, do we?"

"No," I answered. "Lieutenant Guild does have the number here and to my office. He said he would give me call as soon as he knew anything more."

"Good. Good," said the Colonel.

"Colonel MacFay?"

"Yes dear," he replied.

"Colonel, Nicky and I were talking earlier and we thought it would be nice if we could borrow your revolver for a little recreational plinking since we're way out here in the countryside away from everyone."

Since it was Nora asking and the request seemed very plausible, MacFay answered, "Why of course, Nora. Have Nick look in the top right drawer of my desk for the gun and there should be a box of rounds in the lower left. He may have to look around a little for the ammo."

"Oh thank you Colonel. It's been a long time since I've gone target shooting." With a slight welling up in her eyes, and a tentative smile, Nora finished with, "The last time I went shooting was with my father back home in Montana."

"Now, now, Nora. You two go down to the stream behind the house and have fun. You do remember the spot I'm talking about, right?"

"It has been a very long time since we've been back there but yes, I remember. Thanks."

MacFay turned his attention to me. "There is a place behind the house ideal for plinking. It's a fair walk but it leads back to a small nook. You can set things up along the bank down there. Nora's been back there before."

"Thank you, Colonel. This is very nice of you. I was telling Nora how nice it would be to do a little plinking while we were out here away from the city. I used to practice like that all the time when I was younger but since moving to Manhattan I rarely have the chance anymore."

"Now you know why I don't live in the city. Too restrictive for me."

Nora retrieved the revolver and box of ammunition from the desk and gave them to me.

We started down the front steps and turned to the left at the bottom. Walking to the far side of the house we came upon a small workshop building that was no longer used for anything but storage. It wasn't kept locked and Nora turned the door knob and stepped in. The way she walked straight to it and went in, there was no doubt she'd done this before.

"So what's in there?" I asked.

"I thought there might be something in here we could use for targets."

"Oh, I see. Hey, grab that bucket over there," I said, while pointing at it.

"Why do we need a bucket?"

"We'll carry our targets down there in it. We are looking for old cans and bottles, aren't we?"

"That's a good idea. I never thought about that."

"And it can double as a stool if we want."

We spent a while spelunking around the shed and managed to find a handful of old oil cans and our basket of eggs was full. We were finally able to make our way to the shooting range.

"So, you say you've been down here shooting before?" I asked.

"Oh yes. It has been a very long time though. I guess I was just a little girl. I remember one time when we all came back here together. You know, my father and me with Colonel MacFay and Sandra. That seems like a hundred years ago now."

"I see. I guess it's safe then. I mean the backstop and all."

"Oh my yes. The back of the property faces back down the length of the island and there's nothing back there for miles. The water and other homes extend beyond the Colonel's property out to either side. Besides we'll mostly be shooting into a clay embankment anyway."

"Great."

When we got down there I set the bucket down and surveyed the area. It was such a picturesque scene. There was a shallow stream of some width with its water moving briskly around a slight bend. The opposite bank started at the water's edge flat like a sand bar but then rose starkly to expose a wall of hard packed clay. That was our backstop.

"Here's our spot," Nora said.

"I thought it might be. This place is perfect. How do we get over there to set up the cans? Wade over?"

"You could if you like. But there is a little spot right over there you can step across on some stones. That is if the water isn't too high," she answered while pointing to a part of the stream to our right that was just hidden from view because of its turn. "Nicky?"

"Yes."

"Do you think they suspect I had anything to do with this?"

"The only thing I know to tell you is don't worry about anything right now. It's normal in the beginning of anything like this for the police to call in and talk to everyone who knew the victim. It's just their standard procedure to start the file." While holding Colonel MacFay's revolver in my right hand and reaching into my left jacket pocket for the box of rounds I continued with, "Besides, I have things well in hand that should lead me to a major break in the case."

"Oh?"

"Sure. You know how we gumshoes are always sleuthing."

"I'm so glad you're here. Thank you for helping me find who killed my father," Nora said as she blinked back tears. I could only imagine the roller coaster of emotions she was experiencing. Not knowing how she was being scrutinized by the police or other people, where this would lead for her, who actually killed her father and why, and the loss of her father whom she would never spend time with again.

"Believe me when I tell you, I intend to work this case as I have any I've had before. But for now, we're going to do some plinking and enjoy this beautiful weather. Here, take these and you go set them up first. You know where the stepping stones are and where the cans go on the other side. I'll set some things up over here while you do that."

I took the remaining few cans from the bucket and placed them on the ground. I walked to the water's edge and with the aid of one of the cans was able to stand the bucket in the stream and fill it with water. My bullet trap was now in place.

11

By the next morning I still hadn't been called by Guild or the office. Since I had one extra chore for Carol I made the call to her before I started out.

"Good morning, the Nick Charles' Detective Agency, may I help you?"

"Carol? Nick."

"Nick! What's up?"

"Look, you should be getting a call from Lieutenant Guild with the direct telephone number to the medical examiner working on the Finhaden case. I also need you to start the wheels turning on a complete check of the Consolidated Transcontinental Enterprises' financial reports. Go back at least the last six quarters. We'll start with that. Don't forget the loss and earnings as well as banking paperwork."

"Got it. Oh, the Lieutenant gave me that number a little while ago. Want it?"

"Yes please."

"Evergreen 0222. Got it?"

"Yeah, thanks. Gotta' run now. See ya' later."

"Alright Nick. Bye- Oh, one more thing. I almost forgot."

"Yes?"

"You also got a call from Suzette Dewey."

I rolled my eyes. I knew Carol could see it through the phone. "Just leave it on my desk. Thank you."

I disconnected and immediately picked the receiver back up. The operator came back on the line. "Operator, how may I direct your call?"

"Yes operator, can you connect me with Evergreen 0222?"

"One moment please."

After a short wait a voice came back on the line, "Good morning, City of New York Office of Chief Medical Examiner."

"Good morning. This is Nick Charles and I'm calling from Long Island. Is Doctor Sidney Hart in?" I asked.

"Hold please while I check."

Almost as soon as I was placed on hold I heard on the line, "Hello, Doctor Hart."

"Doc, Nick Charles here."

"Nick how've you been?"

"Fine Doc, thanks. Look, Guild called my office and told us you may have something on the Finhaden case."

"Nick, it's good to hear from you again but I just walked in and was trying to pour a cup of coffee. Don't you ever sleep?"

"Not really. I've got too many things to do."

"Yeah, yeah. Hold on a minute and I'll try to find the file. I think it's right on my desk, hang on."

Our conversation lasted much longer than I had anticipated but it was very educational. Doc is definitely one of those guys who is proud of his profession and enjoys detailed conversations about it. He also told me the recovered bullet had been packaged and sent over to the PD lab for further examination regarding ballistics.

"So if you need anything more than that Nick, go see Carnaggio."

"Right Doc. Thanks for everything. I'll be seeing you."

I left Nora with MacFay but I had two bullets fired through MacFay's Colt. After arriving back in Manhattan, I drove straight to Guild's office. Of course, he wasn't there so I drove out to the lab without him. I did leave a message for him he could find me there. By the time I got out to the crime lab Guild had received my message and called out there.

"Hey Nick, what's up?" asked Carnaggio when I walked in.

"Hey Carni, how've you been getting along? It's been a while."

"Yeah Nick, it has. I'm good. Same old thing around here. Guild just called out here for you a little while ago. He's in his office. You know where the phone is."

"Thanks." I made my way to the office and phoned Guild.

"Hello?"

"Lieutenant? Nick. They told me out here at the lab you called."

"That's right. You out there now?"

102

"Yeah, right. I just got here."

"Alright then. Just keep doing what you're doing and hang out there for me. I'm on my way."

"Okay. I'll be here."

After I got off the phone I found Carnaggio back out front. "Carni. Can you do me a favor?"

"What'd'ya need Nick?"

"Do you have the bullet from the Finhaden suicide?"

"Yeah Nick, it just came over a little while ago. I haven't been able to look at it yet. Why?"

"I was just curious. I would like to take a gaze at it."

"Sure. It's still in the box near the scope. I'll come in there with you and set it up."

"Thanks, Carni. Do we even know what caliber it is yet?"

"Well, Aievoli seems to think it's a .32 but we'll confirm that here."

"Doc's usually pretty good at these things."

"Yeah, he is, but we'll mic it here. But you're right. He's seldom wrong unless the bullet is really beat up."

After several minutes he had the spent round set up for viewing. "Are you familiar with the new comparison scope?"

"Yeah. I've read about the new dual comparison scope developed recently by a Philip Gravelle, I believe it was. I haven't really used one but I understand it's going to be a game changer."

"Yes it is. This is the latest model out." he said as he was pulling this and pushing that. "I've got the bullet mounted now but you'll only be able to see it with your left eye. If you want to rotate it just turn this knob here. The other one is for the other side. Since there isn't a comparison bullet you won't need to bother with that one."

"Right."

"One thing I noticed is it's in almost perfect shape. Doc is probably right on the caliber. It also shows me it was from a very low powered handgun loading."

As I settled in to study the bullet removed from Mr. Finhaden, the phone rang. Without looking up I heard Carni walk to the desk and pick up the phone. "Hello," he answered. After a short time, he held the phone to his chest. "Nick, I've got to go pull a couple of case files. You go ahead and check out that bullet while I go down the hall. It'll be alright."

"Thanks, Carni. I'll be right here." I continued to feign interest in the scope as he resumed his telephone conversation. After another minute or so he hung up and walked out of the room. I removed one of MacFay's bullets from my pocket and mounted it in the open side of the scope. I removed the first and repeated the process with the second. There was no doubt all three bullets were fired from the same gun. The striations and tool marks were identical. Since the .32-20 is a small caliber with low power the bullet sent over from the coroner was in very good condition with almost no deformation or distortion. The rifling marks matched my bullets perfectly. After spending a few minutes rotating the samples it seemed there was little doubt that MacFay's gun killed Finhaden. Now all I needed to do was find out who used it.

"Nick, Guild is here."

"Thanks Carni. Thanks for your help with this too," I said as I made my way to the door. I stepped out into the hall and almost bumped into him.

"Nick, let's go back over here to one of the small offices."

"Right."

We entered and I closed the door as Guild walked on around the desk. "Nick, I've got some bad news for you."

"Oh? Do tell."

"I know you've spent a little time with that girl. Finhaden's daughter, Letitia. And you may be starting to like her."

"And?"

"Well Nick, that gun we took from Finhaden's apartment…"

"Yes?"

"Well her print was found on the trigger and a couple of other prints of hers were found on other parts of the gun. It's inconclusive if it was fired but the shell casing was definitely recently fired when we retrieved it. I guess since the .32 caliber bullet probably didn't hit any rifling in the .38 barrel the gun cannot be positively determined to have been fired. Unfortunately, it has not been cleaned in a while and it's hard to tell. But it looks like Nora was the last person to pull the trigger."

"Are you sure? How did you even have her prints on file?"

"About two years ago she was involved in a program at Vassar related to the ROTC Women's Auxiliary. In addition to the military program, her group traveled to Canada for some exchange program thing. A field trip of sorts. It was routine for everyone in these programs to also be fingerprinted for security reasons. She has no criminal record if that's what's bothering you."

"I see."

"Nick. It looks like we'll need to get her back from Colonel MacFay's for questioning. We need your help on this, okay?"

"Right." I didn't know what else to say. I couldn't believe she killed her father and staged a fake suicide. I also knew I had to step back and try to look at everything from a neutral set of eyes. If I could. I may have already let myself get too close to the situation to see it clearly.

"Here is the prelim on the gun. It is a Smith and Wesson Military & Police Model of 1905 .38 Special revolver. It has serial number 544588 with a factory chrome plated finish. It is registered to a Mr. James Finhaden who has a permanent residence in San Francisco, California. The gun was shipped from the factory on March 28, 1927. He has apparently had possession of the weapon for the past year without incident."

"Sounds pretty bland."

"Exactly. No issues with this gun and none with Mr. Finhaden. Then we find someone else's fingerprints on it with him shot in the head. What is your first impression?"

"I see your point."

"Thanks Nick. I know this isn't pleasant for you."

"Lieutenant, can you give me a little time to get her back here? I think I know who you really want to talk to but I'm still working out some details."

"Do tell Nick."

"Besides, she's still out at Colonel MacFay's and it may actually take me a couple of days before I can drive back up there and get her back."

"Who else do you think could be a suspect?"

"Well Lieutenant, we actually have a few possibilities, but I don't want to go off half-cocked. And there may be more than one. Give me a little time on that one too."

"Alright Nick. You've never steered me wrong before so I'll give you the leeway you need. Just keep me in the loop."

"Well lieutenant, you know I will. I always do."

"Thanks Charles."

Lieutenant Guild was a friend and he had helped me on several of my cases even if he didn't realize it. But the clock was ticking on this one and I had to tie up some loose strings quickly. I couldn't put him off indefinitely. It was time to get back to the office and sift through the boring paperwork to connect some of the administrative dots.

12

I wasn't quite ready to completely pull this thing together so I went along with the flow for now. It didn't square that Nora fired the fatal shot since the bullets I brought back from MacFay's matched up to the bullet recovered from Finhaden at the coroner's office. If a .32-20 had been fired through a .38 Special bore there shouldn't be any rifling on the bullet. These three rounds had very distinct striations indicating a very snug fit in a proper barrel. The science and technique of bullet comparison evidence is still fairly new especially as it takes in the comparison scope. But I was convinced the murder weapon belonged to Colonel MacFay and was not the revolver owned by Mr. Finhaden. If it were Colonel MacFay, why? That didn't really make sense either. He knew well he had nothing to gain from it. There was Nora to step in per their survivor clause. Unless of course he intended to set her up or kill her too.

I checked in with my office and Carol told me Clyde Wynant had stopped by. "So, what is he up to today?" I asked.

"He stopped by this morning with his secretary, Miss Wolf. He just wanted to know if you found out anything from Chicago. I told him I don't know anything about your cases but I'd tell you he came by."

"Good. I guess I'll detour by his place. Thanks." Before making the trip over to Clyde's place I stopped at my apartment and called Chicago.

"Trans-American Detective Agency, Chicago Bureau, may I help you?"

"Hey, Carla, it's Nick. Nick Charles in New York."

"Nick. Well, how've you been getting along?"

"I can't complain dear. How've you been?"

"Well, you know how it is."

"Look, I need to talk to Jimmy White. Is he around?"

"Hold on sweetie, I'll check."

After a brief wait she came back online. "Hold on Nick, I'm switching you to his office. Bye."

"Thanks Carla. Talk to you later."

"Nick?"

"Jimmy. How've you been doing pal?"

"Doin' good, doin' good. So what's up?"

"Look I need a favor.

"Sure. Name it."

"Great. Nothing big. I just need you to check on a name and phone number there in Chicago for me. I need to know if this guy is real or not."

"Sure. No problem."

"He's supposed to be a dentist by the name of Rosewood and his telephone number is Underwood-354. Any little thing you can drum up would be greatly appreciated."

"You bet. I should be able to run that down for you by tomorrow."

"Great. Just call my office and leave it with Carol. She'll get it on out to me. Thanks."

With that started I decided to go ahead and call Wynant. I was planning to talk with him in person but he's a little nutty and I'd rather put that off.

After calling Clyde and pushing that matter back I called MacFay's next. After the obligatory greetings and conversation with the Colonel, he put Nora on the line.

"Hello?"

"Nora?"

"Yes."

"Nick."

"Oh, Nicky! How are you?"

"I'm well, thanks. And you?"

"I'm okay I guess."

"Look Nora, I need to ride back out there and speak with you again."

"Oh?"

"Yeah, it's more about your father."

"Oh."

"May I call on you tomorrow afternoon? I may even come out late and need to spend the night out there again."

"That's fine with me and I'm sure I can answer for the Colonel as well. I'll let him know you're coming."

"That's fine. I need to go now and tend to some other work but I'll see you tomorrow. Take care of yourself and good night."

"You too Nicky. Bye."

A part of me felt a little guilty. Like I had lied to her even though I hadn't. Being sneaky is more like it I guess which I confess never bothered me a bit when dealing with anyone else. I was beginning to think I really did like this girl. After all she was different. As far as my rational thinking being affected by it; I did not think so. There seemed to be several things coming together in my mind encompassing a slightly larger circle of potential suspects. And with a little more foot work, I was counting on the physical evidence to link that up. I needed one more trip to the scene. Mr. Finhaden's suite at the Commodore. Guild told me the apartment was still sealed by order of the NYPD and would be made available to me when I was able to work it in. I was off to the Commodore again.

Entering the lobby, I made my way directly to the front desk. "Good morning," I said to the gentleman behind the counter.

"Good morning sir. I'll be right with you," he replied while he placed mail into the pigeon holes on the back wall.

I took the opportunity to take in the lobby and watch the activity for a moment.

"Mr. Charles, how are you this morning. It's a pleasure to see you again," came another voice from a different direction. I turned to greet Mr. Sullivan, the hotel manager. As I reached out and shook his hand I replied, "Well, thank you. And yourself?"

"I'm fine, thank you for asking. So, how may we be of assistance to you today?"

"That room where Mr. Finhaden was found; I believe Suite 714, it is still taped off, right?"

"Why yes sir it is. No one has entered it since the police blocked it off. Lieutenant Guild asked us to leave it undisturbed for you. Were you needing to see it today?"

"Well, I was just out walking my dog and suddenly turned the corner and found myself out front. Then I thought; well, since I'm here I might as well get this over with."

"Very good sir. I'll get the key. Oh, I am sorry though, no pets are allowed in the Commodore."

"Pet? He's no pet. I don't even really like him. You see, this is Asta. He's a highly trained police dog used in forensic investigations. I have to take him up and use him to help check the scene. If it were up to me he wouldn't even be here but, well, you know how it is."

"A police dog? Well, I guess he can go upstairs with you then. I've never heard of that though."

"Oh yes. You know New York. They're always on the cutting edge using new methods and all."

"I guess you're right. Here's the key Mr. Charles."

"Thank you my good man. We shall return shortly. Come along Asta, we have work to do."

As we stepped on the elevator the operator took a long look at Asta. "Sir, you know dogs aren't allowed."

"It's alright. He's my seeing eye dog."

"Oh, I'm sorry. I didn't realize."

"That's quite alright. Seven please."

When the elevator stopped and the operator pulled open the door I stepped off and the leash became taut. I stopped just outside the door and looked back at Asta. "Come on boy. Let's go."

"I thought you said he was a Seeing Eye dog," said the elevator operator.

"Did I say that? No, I meant he is a rare oppidan blood hound and he's tracking the extremely rare and elusive New York City Hare. We're trying to make history here today and I need your complete discretion so as not to alert and alarm the residents. That would scare it away."

"Wow. Really? I had no idea. Okay mister" he said. After a moment of contemplation he continued with, "What's oppidan?"

Once at the apartment door I just stood there for a minute taking in the entranceway. You can never rush these things. Details. Take your time and take in the details. These are what tell the story. How did the suspect get in? No one stopped at the desk and asked for a key. Nora was with me and she used her key to get in as I walked back to the elevators. And it certainly wasn't Mr. Finhaden.

Okay, the apartment is at the corner, where one hallway turns off the other. There are stairs at each end of both hallways. I took out my flashlight and shined it into the lock. The brass keyway had small shiny scratches that stood out from the duller finish. I quickly checked several other locks nearby and found no sign of scratches on any of them. This could only indicate that whoever went into this apartment that night also knows how to pick locks. These are the tell-tale signs of picking tools being used. The combination of a rake for the internal pins and a tension tool to turn the cylinder once the pins correctly line up and unlock. Our suspect has probably worked as a locksmith.

After spending some time in the hall, I finally let myself in. Asta went his way and I went mine. I made a fairly quick cursory walk-through of the entire apartment just in case something jumped out at me but everything seemed to be normal and in place. As is normally the case I was going to have to work at finding anything. One thing I did know though was if someone came in here that night they left something behind. It may be small. It may be minute. But they left something. We had to find it.

Walking through the bedroom I methodically checked every quarter again hoping for that missed clue when I stopped to watch Asta. He seemed to be honed in on something but I couldn't tell what it was. He was sniffing and pawing at the bedroom door frame leading back out. Walking toward him I noticed it was just one small area he seemed interested in. Even with good daylight shining through the windows I still couldn't see anything unusual. That is until I used my flashlight again. Only now with the room well-lit and a brighter light focused on the area I could make out a portion of the doorframe about two to three feet from the floor that was a shade darker than the rest of the paint in the area. Then it hit me. This was the same spot that briefly caught my eye when I was up here with Nora the night it happened. I had completely forgotten about it since then. Something like that wasn't like me. I walked back out to the desk looking for a small envelope. The top of the desk seemed to be in very neat order with little on it. I sat down and started checking the drawers. Finally, in the bottom right drawer I found some envelopes.

As I pushed the drawer closed, my eye caught sight of a very nice ladies silk handkerchief near the opposite corner of the desktop. For some reason my gaze became fixed on it. Why was that there? It seemed so out of place. I finally picked it up and took a closer look. Holding it spread open with both hands I could see a white on white embroidered monogram embellished with a flourish. This was made of very fine material and appeared to be high end craftsmanship. The monogram was a little difficult to see but it looked to be an overlapping triple 'SMS'. That seemed out of place, so I placed it in my jacket pocket.

I walked back to the bedroom door with the envelope and with my penknife I gently scraped the surface of Asta's spot. When I finished collecting the surface material the paint seemed to match again. The hotel can thank me later.

Resigned to the fact the apartment was combed through extensively and I would probably not find another clue, Asta and I left. I walked across the lobby and stopped at the front desk to return the key. "Thank you very much for all your help," I said as I extended my hand holding the key.

Taking the key from me the desk clerk replied, "Thank you Mr. Charles. It was our pleasure to be of assistance to the police and you during this unpleasant time. Please do not hesitate to call on us again."

"Thank you," I said and then looked down. "Let us be on our way now Asta" with his answering with a yip.

13

We traveled back out to see my friend Carni at the crime lab. Walking in the front door I met the front desk receptionist at her station. "Good morning Beth."

Looking up from her work she replied warmly, "Nick. How are you?"

"Looks like I'm sitting pretty these days. If I felt better I'd have to slap myself. And how have you been getting along?"

"I'm still here."

"Hey, how about a cup of that joe?"

"Sure. Just made it. Help yourself."

As I walked around the counter to the pot I asked her, "Is Carni around?"

"He's out back last I saw. Go on back and find him. He never answers that intercom anyway. I don't think he's ever at his desk."

"Thanks," I said as I sat the pot down. I made my way back to his domain and true to form, he was not sitting at his desk.

"Carni," I called out.

"Nick, come on in. What's cooking today?" came a voice.

As I walked further into the lab area, he made his way in from another part of the building. I pulled the envelope from my inside jacket pocket. "Carni, I have some scrapings here from the bedroom door frame of the Commodore where Finhaden was killed. Can you test this stuff and tell me if there's anything besides wood or paint here?"

"I should be able to. Do you know what you're looking for in it?"

"Not really. Could be anything. But since we're looking into a shooting what about anything related to guns?"

"I can check it for GSR right now."

"Terrific."

Carni took my sample and worked his magic and in a few minutes told me, "I'm not sure this test result can be called conclusive. It is a little old and there are other chemicals mixed in but I think I can safely tell you there is some type of gunshot residue in this."

"Really? What other chemicals do you think are in this?"

"Nothing unusual really. I'd say mostly the makeup of the paint."

"I don't know what I'd do without you my friend. Let me buy you lunch."

"It's a deal. Oh, I almost forgot too. You remember asking me a while back about that big Consolidated Transcontinental mill fire in New Jersey?"

"Oh yeah. That was so long ago I almost forgot about it myself."

"Well they finally called day before yesterday with some preliminary stuff. It seems this thing was done a lot like that school bombing last year over near Lansing, Michigan."

"Someone brought in a bomb?"

"More or less. It was a truck packed with dynamite attached to a time delayed fuse. When they realized they were dealing with a truck bomb they called in the Army Explosive guys from Camp Dix. They rallied there and went over to the site. Those guys really know their stuff and put the pieces back together."

"Yeah, I saw a little of what they do when we were in Europe."

"The only good thing about this one is no one was killed. They had two workers injured because they were on the other side of the building when it went off. A security guard remembered seeing a pickup truck enter the employee parking area but thought it was only a worker running late to start his shift. The same guy reported seeing a car leaving the same parking area about fifteen minutes later. He did say he thought this was unusual since it was well into the work shift."

"It sounds like they hired the right guy to watch over the place."

We finished up our conversation and left for lunch. Things were beginning to form a timeline for me and some of the dots were starting to connect.

"How about a dog?" he asked.

"What about a dog?" I replied.

"Red hots! I'm really busy and there's a great dog wagon down on the corner. I think

119

Nathan's brings 'em up in the morning. We can just walk down in two minutes."

"I'm game. Let's go."

As we strolled down the walk the conversation continued. "So we're basically talking about a pre-rigged truck bomb here?"

"That's right Nick. They sent a packet by courier with copies of their reports, diagrams, and photographs. When you have the time you're more than welcome to take a look at the stuff but I have to keep the originals in house."

"That's fine. I don't need to take anything with me. Do you know if they ID'd the truck?"

"They did. I can't remember anything about it right now. I do remember it had been reported stolen a few days before the bombing. Big surprise there, huh?"

"I'm curious about where it was stolen from. And from whom. I'll take a quick look at that stuff when we get back if that's alright."

"Not a problem. It's sitting on my desk."

After we enjoyed our frankfurter gourmet meal, I had a chance to read over the New Jersey file. There were a number of things there that really caught my eye. Heading out I asked, "Would it be possible to have a few things copied and sent over to the office?"

"Shouldn't be a problem but it will take a few days. Just stop on your way out and tell Beth what you need."

"Thanks pal. I owe you."

"You always owe me. If I ever collected I could retire."

14

After leaving the crime lab I went back to my office. Carol handed me a note with a telephone number scrawled on it. "Jimmy White in Chicago wants you to call him back when you get in."

"Thanks Carol."

After our call connected I started the conversation. "Jimmy? Nick. What'cha got?"

"Nick, good to hear from you again. Look, I've got a few little things you may be interested in. That Rosewood guy. Well we can't find him here."

"Really?"

"Yeah, but get this now. We did find that telephone number and it belongs to a Doctor Reinhardt Meyer. And he's not a dentist but an oculist."

"Okay."

"It gets better. It looks like this guy had some odd fascination with the crime bosses and got mixed up with one of the gangs here. I'm not sure what he got out of it other than the excitement. I mean, the guy's a doctor. It wasn't for the money."

"And."

"Well, just last week he met up with a couple of other gangsters at a south side garage in the morning and they all got killed in a hit by another gang. He's dead. If your guy's Rosewood is this Doctor Meyer his troubles are over."

"Thanks Jimmy. I think you just wrapped this little thing up for me. Let me know if I can return the favor."

"Right. See ya' later."

I toggled the intercom and called, "Carol, see if you can get Clyde Wynant on the line."

"Yes sir."

I needed to head home and get ready for another few days running back up to MacFay's place. I was about to leave for my place when Carol buzzed back. "Mr. Charles?"

"Yes."

"Mrs. Wynant is on the line."

"Thank you, Carol."

I set my hat down and picked up the phone. "Mimi? Nick Charles here. Is Clyde around?"

"Nick. How have you been? It's so nice to hear from you."

"Mimi, I need to see Clyde. I have some information for him. Is he home today?"

"You can tell me and I'll let him know."

"He asked me to give it to him personally."

"Well alright then. He's here but out back. You can come on over and see him then."

"Thanks Mimi. I'll be over in a little while. Bye."

I picked up my hat and coat and I was on my way back out the door. "Carol, I'm off to Wynant's place. I'll probably head on home when I'm finished with him."

"Alright. I'll be here if you need anything."

"Thanks."

Since Mimi told me Clyde was around I foolishly believed her and drove over to see him. I was able to park directly in front of their flat. Only a few steps from the car I was knocking on their door. Mimi answered and opened the door just a few inches at first. Then she swung the door completely open.

"Oh Nick, it's so good to see you again. Won't you come in?" she said while batting her eyes and smiling.

I stepped inside and closed the door as Mimi stepped back from the doorway. "Thanks Mimi. Where's Clyde?"

"Oh. Clyde? Uh, well, he left."

"He left? Didn't you tell him I called?"

"Uh, yes. Yes, I did. He said he would be back in a few minutes. Can I get you something to drink?"

"Mimi. Clyde hasn't been here all day, has he? He wasn't here when I called, was he?"

"Nick, for all I know he's off with that tramp Julia Wolf. I don't care if he ever comes back. She can keep him" she replied now with a stark scowl on her face.

"Mimi—"

"Nick, won't you come on in and take a load off your feet? Have a seat," she said as her face contorted back to what had been earlier at the door. "Mimi, I'm not staying."

"Oh Nick, you won't regret it if you do."

"Oh yes, Mimi, I will," I said as I made my way back to the door.

"Nick, please stay. I'll behave."

"Mimi, you know, I need to call over to the Herald Tribune and get Don Marquis to have Archy write about you. You're some screwy dame. How you and Clyde are still married is anybody's guess. You're both mad as a cut snake. I've got to go."

When I got back to the door I grabbed the knob and pulled the door open. "Mimi, just tell Clyde I came by. You have a good evening." "Nick!" Clyde called out from down the sidewalk as I reached for the door handle.

"Clyde" I replied while walking back around the car to the sidewalk.

"So what brings you by?"

"I got a little information from Chicago I thought you would like to hear."

"Oh? You learn anything new?"

"I have. It seems your crazy business partner may be out of commission now."

"Oh?"

"My folks in Chicago think Rosewood wasn't his real name but the phone number you gave me was good. It was to a doctor named Meyers. It seems he's not a dentist either but rather an oculist. I think it's the same guy because this Doctor Meyers was also mixed up with the mobsters there and got himself shot."

"No kidding?"

"He's dead. It seems a few guys were to meet some bootleggers in a south side garage to work out a deal on a truckload of hooch. This idiot doctor went along with 'em and once inside these bootleggers and a couple of cops drew down on 'em and stood 'em against a wall. Then they just gunned 'em down."

"What?"

"Yep. Just executed all of 'em standing against a brick wall. I'm betting it's the same fella you were dealing with and you won't hear from him again. Keep me posted if you do have another episode with him and we'll try something different."

"Thanks Nick. That's swell. I feel better already."

"Anytime Clyde. Talk to you later. Gotta' go now. Bye."

I got back in the car and pulled away about as quickly as I could. With Mimi in the mood she was in I didn't want to be anywhere near that place when he went in.

I think I was able to get Clyde satisfied and now I could focus more on this murder case. He's a strange one but a good customer. I was running later than I originally wanted to but things happen. It was time to get the car loaded and ready for the road. I had to talk with Nora again and of course Guild had been wanting to see her too.

I checked back in with Carol. "I'll be heading back to Long Island and will probably be gone at least overnight. Could you call Lieutenant Guild and let him know I'm headed back up to Colonel MacFay's?"

"You know I will."

"Thanks Carol. And tell him I'll get back with him as soon as I get back."

"Okay. Be careful."

"Thanks. See ya' later."

15

Pulling up to the front of MacFay's place I was met at the door by Nora and Colonel MacFay. The hired help must have sounded the alarm when I came through the gate. And I was beginning to get used to the staff toting in the bag and parking the car. Just as I started up the steps Colonel MacFay said, "Well Nick, my boy, you're looking well. I hope your drive up was uneventful."

"Yes Colonel, it was a pleasant cruise through the country side. Now that I've spent almost two boring, stone sober hours alone in a car, do you remember the way to the bar?"

"Of course, of course. Right this way my boy."

"And hello to you too," I said to Nora as I reached the top of the steps and started into the door.

"Hi Nicky. I'm glad to see you again."

"You say that now but wait 'til I tell why I'm really out here."

"Oh?"

"It'll wait. Let's get that rye now."

"Alright. You remember where everything is. Lead the way."

I followed Colonel MacFay back into the library. Nora held back and walked with me. The Colonel walked into the study while we were still in the foyer. I stopped and turned to Nora. She stopped walking and with furrowed brows asked, "What is it Nicky?"

"Nora?"

"Yes Nicky."

"Uh, Nora…"

"What is it?"

"Never mind. Let's get in there before he comes back out here."

"Alright."

We strolled on in and MacFay was already getting our drinks ready. He's a fine man and very hospitable. I realized after several visits out here I want to be just like him when I grow up.

"Here Nick. It was Straight Rye neat, wasn't it?"

"Yes sir. You remembered right. Thank you."

"And here's yours Nora."

"Thank you Colonel," she said.

Colonel MacFay continued, "So Nick, what really brings you back out here so soon?"

"Well Colonel, you know how these investigations can be?"

"Not really. What's up?"

"Well we just need to tie up a few last loose strings. I think we're getting pretty close to wrapping this thing up but like I said, there are just a few little loose strings we need to put to bed."

"I see. Can you say anything more than something about strings yet?"

"Colonel, to be honest I'd rather just enjoy the drink, conversation, and the evening right now. There's plenty of time to talk shop later."

"I understand. And I can't say I blame you. It is late in the day and I'm sure you'd rather just unwind right now."

16

Morning came and we were all seated around the breakfast table having our coffee, waiting for our plates to be brought out. Colonel MacFay chimed in again asking about developments. He's not really a very patient man when it comes to something he is genuinely interested in.

"Alright," I said. "There are a few odd developments with this case. I'm still not completely clear in my head as to the timeline and connections but the picture is coming into focus. I can tell you we have more or less come to the conclusion this is not a suicide."

"Then what?" asked the Colonel.

"If not a suicide then what else? A murder."

"Murder? Are you sure?"

"Yes."

"Any suspects developed?"

"Yes. At least in my mind. I'm not exactly sure what the police have in mind. That's partly why I'm back out here. Nora, Lieutenant Guild asked me if I could drive out here and bring you back to the city."

"He did?"

"Yes. It's nothing to be concerned about but he wants to interview you for his file. You remember the night everyone was in the apartment we didn't have a chance to talk to him. You and I left in the middle of everything and he didn't get a chance to talk with you at all. They really need to speak with you to clear up a few things. I mean, you did live there with your father and all."

"Nicky. You're starting to run on. Tell me. Am I a suspect? Does Guild think I did it?"

"I'm not sure. Maybe. But trust me; even if he does I know it wasn't you and I think I can prove who did."

"What do you mean, 'I think'?"

"I'm pretty sure I can, yes."

"You do!? Well, who then!?"

"I can't say just yet. You'll have to trust me for now."

"Alright Nicky. I guess I really have no choice."

"I know you'd rather ride back to New York with me than one of his guys."

"Yes I would. I've seen them talking to other people and they don't seem to me to be friendliest folks. Some of them must have had some pretty harsh potty training,"

"That is true, but I was thinking it was simply because it would be me you'd be riding with. Those guys aren't really that bad."

"Oh. I'm sorry. Yes, you're right. It shall be a pleasant ride spending time talking with you again. You must excuse me. My mind is wandering off somewhere else these days."

"It's no wonder. Think nothing of it. Look, I'll talk with the Colonel for a while and let you pack a bag, or two, or three. Anyway, go pack and let me know when you're ready."

Nora started upstairs and I walked to the counter and poured myself another cup of coffee. "Colonel, what is this? I mean the coffee. This is the best coffee I think I've ever had?"

"It probably is the best you've had. I have a friend who lives most of the year in Hawai'i not far from Mauna Kea. I see him about once a year usually at some conference. Anyway, a few years ago he brought me about a pound of this stuff from Hawai'i when he came to New England for some growers' convention. Did you know the best wrapper leaves for premium hand-rolled cigars in the world are grown in Connecticut, Massachusetts, and Vermont?"

"I did not know that."

"Me neither. I thought they all came from the Caribbean or Cuba. But they wrap the finished cigar with these Connecticut Shade wrapper leaves. Somebody is always experimenting with growing things in different types of soil. Anyway, I think they're going to experiment with that Kona region coffee up here too."

"Kona?"

"Oh yes, that's what you're drinking. I was told someone brought some South American plants to the Kona Region of Hawai'i in the early 1800's to see how it would grow there. It turned out that the combination of climate and soil found there makes the perfect coffee. I like it so well I have to occasionally order some from one of the plantations down there."

"Yes, I can see why. Changing the subject, you've spent more time around Nora than I have. How is she holding up to all this?"

"I do feel bad for her. She's been taking this pretty rough. Oh, she puts up a good front, mind you. She's a very strong willed young lady. I guess she picked that up from her father. But you can tell."

"This would be hard on anyone. I'm not surprised. But you're right. In the short time I've known her I can tell she's pretty darn independent. She certainly speaks her mind."

"And you wouldn't have it any other way."

"What?"

"You heard me."

"What do you mean?"

"Nick, I'm old but not blind or stupid. She needs someone to lean on now more than ever. Oh sure, I'm here for her and I always will be. I've said too much already. I don't get involved in other people's personal business. Just think about what I said."

"I have Colonel. I think I would like that job. She is different."

"And she likes you too, my boy."

"Oh?"

"I've said too much. You'll have to find out the rest on your own."

About that time Nora stuck her head in the door. "Nicky, I think I'm ready."

"Alright Nora, I'll be right there."

"Oh, there's no need to come get anything. The bags are being taken out front now."

"I keep forgetting about that."

17

With Colonel MacFay still seated and me standing near the coffee pot I sat my cup down and walked toward the door. Just as I started out the door I stopped and looked back. "Colonel, thanks for everything. No need to get up. I'll get Nora to the city and back in no time. I'll take care of everything."

"I know you will my boy. I know you will. Come back anytime."

"Thanks." With my final word I turned back to the door and left him sitting alone at the table.

In the hallway with Nora I asked her, "Are you sure you have everything you need? This may take a couple of day."

"Oh yes. Besides we do still have the apartment at the Commodore and I have more things there."

"I don't know why but I completely forgot about that Commodore apartment. I took it for granted after I left they would clean it and rent it back out like any other hotel room."

"Oh no Nicky. Father keeps that suite on retainer. It's a leased apartment we keep year-round. It's always available for either of us when we come into the city. Did you say, when you left the apartment?"

"Oh, uh, yes. Yes I did."

"Did you go back there again? After the police left?"

"As a matter of fact, I did. I was going to go more into that on our ride back."

After Colonel MacFay's valet brought my car back up front and they loaded our luggage Nora and I finally left. It didn't take long for the conversation to turn back to the Commodore.

"So, you went back to the apartment again?"

"Yeah, Me and Asta."

"Asta? Who is Asta?"

"Asta is my dog. And he's smarter than most people. You'll have an opportunity to meet him when we get back this time. I value his opinion too. Hopefully he'll like you."

"And if he doesn't?"

"For some reason I believe I'm as good a judge of character as he is. If that is true, you have nothing to worry about."

"Why would I have to worry about that anyway?"

She knew exactly what I was talking about and had painted me in a corner. Or as she would have put it; I stepped right into it. And I did too.

"Look, I found a couple of things I wanted to talk to you about before we get back to Guild."

"I want to talk about Asta."

"Do you always get your way?"

"Usually."

136

"I see."

"Oh," I reached into my jacket pocket and pulled out the silk handkerchief I found at the Commodore when Asta and I were looking it over. "I found this on the floor earlier and was wondering if you lost it,"

She reached out and took it from me and looked it over. I watched for any kind of reaction or expression, but it was difficult while I was driving. I couldn't tell. She seemed unimpressed. Handing it back to me she said, "I'm afraid not. It's very nice but it isn't mine. It must belong to one of your girlfriends."

"Sorry, no."

"Have you asked them yet?"

"You're a pistol, you know it?"

"What do you mean?"

"Look…" I froze. I've never done that before. What was going on here?

"Look at what?"

"Nora, there are some things I would like to talk with you about but now is probably not the right time. We need to stay focused on your father's murder. We need to get your part in the investigation wrapped up and I need to finish tying up the loose ends on finding the killer."

"You're right Nicky. I'm sorry. I'll try to be more serious. What do you want me to do?"

"Tell me about the day your friend Sandra came to visit you at the apartment before your father was killed."

"Oh, alright. Well, let's see. Nothing really. She came up and I let her in. We talked and then left to go shopping. Nothing special. Just some girl stuff, you know."

"Okay. Let me walk you back through it, alright?"

"Well, okay."

Over the next hour of riding back to New York I was able to walk her through what had happened that day, step by step. What I picked up on was very interesting. Nora gave me a great deal of information that was worthy of a deeper look and some follow up work. And at the same time I'm sure she really had no idea what she was telling me. That's the way I wanted it too. Since she had known Sandra for so many years and she felt they were as close as sisters I certainly didn't want to upset her or put her on the defensive. And if she got the impression I was accusing Sandra of anything and it turned out she had nothing to do with it my name would be Mudd with her. This was definitely an area to tread lightly.

"So the two of you did talk about your father's gun that day?"

"Well, yes. Like I told you, she saw it in the drawer and said something about it and I picked it up and offered it to her to look at. She didn't want anything to do with it and then we left."

"Okay. I'm just trying to go over everything carefully for when Guild interviews you. You need to be as honest with him as you can be. Sometimes those guys get a little ill-tempered if they think somebody is trying to play 'em."

"Oh. Right. I see. Thanks Nicky."

I was beginning to a get a much clearer picture now. I still had a lot of footwork to put in though.

Later in the day we made it back to the Commodore and I helped Nora with her bags. As we stepped off the elevator and started down the hall I asked her, "Okay Nora, let's start here and slowly walk me through what you did that night after I walked back to the elevator."

"Alright. I just opened the door... I unlocked the door with my key while you were still with me."

"Yes. I remember. Go ahead."

"When you turned to walk away I pushed the door open and walked in closing the door behind me. The desk lamp was on and a very dim light could be seen in Father's room. His door was ajar and that seemed unusual to me. He usually has it shut. So I just looked in on him but something didn't feel right."

"Oh?"

"You know. Nothing I could really put my finger on but something was just not right. I pushed the door open and stepped in and in the dim light I could see the gun lying in the floor. That's when I pushed the light switch button on the wall next to the door. When the ceiling light came on I could see he'd been shot."

"Yes?"

"I just ran back to the door screaming. I was hoping you were still there."

"Anything else?"

"No. It was really all just a blur. And the blur just got worse as the morning went on."

"Alright. Let's go on in and make some coffee."

In just a little while we were sitting in the front room sipping our cups of coffee and continuing the review. I kept thinking about the spot on the door frame and the handkerchief. I couldn't decide yet if I should tell Nora about what I knew. As of now I thought I'd just sit on it. "So you've known Sandra pretty much your whole life. How long have you known Duie?"

"Oh, Duie? Since just before they got married. I don't really know much about him except he's German. She met him over there."

"Really?"

"Yeah. She went over right after she graduated on some fact-finding thing for her father. They were always looking at expanding or diversifying. Especially Colonel MacFay. That sort of thing seems to just come natural to him."

"So that's what brought Sandra and Duie together? Business interests?"

"I guess you could say that. It sure didn't take long for things to heat up though. In just a few months she had him moving to the States and they got married."

"I guess you could call that a merger."

"I always thought it was genuine though. I mean Duie already ran a very successful business on his own. He wasn't looking through her at the money and she certainly didn't need his."

"I see what you mean."

So now I had a little background on those two and some more places to look regarding our friend Duie. Most of his operations, banking, and paper trails would be found in Europe. It looked like I would have to be calling in some favors.

"Nora."

"Yes Nick."

"I've enjoyed the company and the coffee, but I think I should be going."

"No Nicky. Stay a little longer. What about supper? I know you haven't eaten today."

"No really. There are a few things I need to do before calling it a day. But I'll be back about ten in the morning for brunch. Be ready to go by then."

"Alright, I will. Don't stand me up."

"You're kidding, right?"

She followed me to the door to see me out. There was that awkward face to face moment as I put my hand on the door knob. I had been struggling the entire time to keep my distance and stay professional. At least until all this was over. As I started to turn the door knob she leaned in and kissed me. I let the knob go and kissed back. When we came up for air she simply stepped back and without skipping a beat she asked, "So how is Chelsea's on the Square? I don't think I've eaten there before?"

"You'll love the Eggs Benedict Champagne brunch." This time I didn't linger and turned the door knob. "You have a good evening and I'll be back in the morning."

"Goodbye Nicky."

18

I checked in with my office around eight the next morning. "Carol, I need you to set up some business filing and bank records research for a German firm by the name of Schlusser Exportieren GmbH. They bank exclusively with the Reichsbank so I understand it may take a while."

"Boss, you know that's gonna' be a piece of cake. Check back in a little while."

"That's my girl. I need loss and earning statements and balance sheets for the past eight quarters. I'm off now. I'll call later today. Thanks."

"It's as good as done. Behave yourself out there now."

"Why start now?"

Now that I had those wheels turning I took off for the Commodore. It looked like I was going to time it just about right. I finally made it there and on time to boot. As Nora and I started off for our brunch date I started the conversation with, "So have you had a chance to make any arrangements yet? For your father?"

"As soon as I'm freed up with what the police need from me we'll travel back to San

Francisco by train. The travel plans are all but done. I still have to get things in order back home. I have been able to speak with Father Cariss by phone and get some preliminary things started."

"Good. Let me know if I can do anything to help."

"I'll let you know. Thanks."

"I called Guild earlier this morning and told him we'd be by about two. That'll give him time to get squared away and back from lunch. If he takes a lunch break."

Nora and I continued our conversation as we stepped off the elevator and started across the lobby. I definitely had the impression that as far as this case was concerned she was tapped out. I knew she was straight up about what she was saying and this thing with Guild was just jumping through hoops. The pieces of this puzzle were starting to come together and it wouldn't be long before I sat down for a serious pow-wow with Guild. We were walking past a bank of phones and I couldn't resist. "Look Nora, I need to make a quick call before we get out of here. I'll just be a minute."

"Alright."

Something told me to check in before we got out of pocket.

"Carol. It's Nick."

"Oh Nick, I'm glad you called. I've got some hot stuff for you on those records you wanted pulled from Germany."

Carol went on to fill me in on the high points. She was right. This was developing into some interesting turns. "Carol, make some copies and lock up the originals you have. I'll be by as soon as I can get freed up and collect 'em from you. Thanks sweetheart." It was starting to look like our friend Duie wasn't all straight laced and above board. There was more checkered about him than a table cloth. That was one thing that made Carol invaluable. She would always shortcut my reading and research time on important cases.

Nora and I covered the last block to the river front on foot. When we made it to Chelsea's I asked, "So, do you want to go in or would you prefer to take in the view?"

"Oh Nicky, it's such a lovely day. Let's sit outside."

"That's fine."

When we got to the door I asked the maître d' to seat us on the terrace. We had a great view of the skyline across the river and the passing boat traffic. Spring had arrived in New York. The waiter came to the table. "Good morning. May I bring you anything sir?"

"Please bring us coffee to start with. Nora, would you care for anything else?"

"Oh, just water would be fine too."

"Yes, water here too, Thanks."

"Lemon?"

"Oh yes, please."

"Very good. Will you be needing a menu?"

"No. That won't be necessary. We know what we'll be ordering."

"Do you wish to order now?"

"I suppose we could. Just send out two Eggs Benedict Champagne Brunch specials with a side plate of fresh fruit. Did I forget anything Nora?"

"No Nicky. That sounds fine."

"Thank you," I said to the waiter and he departed. "Now Nora, what do you think of Chelsea's on the Square?"

"It all looks so lovely. I only hope the food is as good."

"It is. I promise you won't be disappointed." After a short pause I changed the subject with, "Nora. You know they're looking at this thing with your father as a homicide now, right? The suicide angle has pretty much been ruled out."

"I thought so."

"Do you have any idea who your father's enemies are? Who could possibly have wanted to do this?"

"Don't you think I've been thinking about that? It's all I've been thinking about. I can't think of a single person who would have wanted to do anything like this. I wish I did know."

We finished breakfast and caught up with Guild in his office. I managed to get him off to the side and let him know I had some rather important developments to go over with him when he finished interviewing Nora. I'm not sure but that may have also shortened the interview which was also a good thing.

The lieutenant and Nora stepped out of his office after a very short time. Nora said to me, "That sure was brief. I'm not sure why we even came down here."

"That's fine. I told you they interview everyone remotely connected to the victim as a matter of routine. He needed it for the file, that's all. Just have a seat over there and wait for me. I need to go over a few things with him and we'll head out. I'll only be a minute."

"Alright Nicky. I'll be here."

I walked in Guilds office. He was already seated behind the desk. "Coffee?"

"No thanks, I've had more than my share today."

"So what is this bombshell you have?"

"Are you up on your international current affairs?"

"I guess so. Why?"

"Have you been keeping up with that little ruckus down in Nicaragua?"

"Sort of. Why?"

"Okay, here it is. You know Colonel MacFay's son-in-law, that Duie Schlusser from Germany?"

"Yeah. We didn't see any flags there."

"Well it seems our Duie is of a well-connected family and was well trained as a sturmtruppe serving in the old Imperial Deutsches Reich up until the war's end."

"Yeah. I already have that."

"His service record is not at issue but the practical training he received as a soldier could be. I think the unit he was in was something on the order of a commando group. They trained on automatic weapons, improvised explosives, and escape and

146

evasion tactics. The last even involved learning the locksmithing trade. As in lock picking."

"Sounds like a very talented mug. Go on."

"Yes indeed. We need to get his military records for a better look into that but listen to this. You know we've had a military presence in Nicaragua for a much longer period. Our marines were down there years before we entered the war in Europe.

"Yeah, that's right."

"The Nicaraguans finally held a legitimate Presidential election in '24 after all that civil war stuff in the teens."

"Charles, are we going somewhere with this?"

"The U.S. government withdrew our troops in early 1925 thinking things were now stable but as soon as all American forces were gone the former president launched a coup d'etat."

"That's right. I did read about that in the papers."

"Right. The coup toppled the elected government and the whole mess devolved into a full scale civil war again."

"Yeah, that's right. How is that our problem?"

"Well it seems our Duie actually made his fortune in arms sales and as a mercenary helping whichever side had money during the 1925 coup and then the year long civil war in '26 and '27. His Schlusser Exportieren GmbH seems to be nothing more than a shell company to launder money."

"Oh. I see. How did you get this Charles?"

"Trade secret. Now if nothing else Lieutenant, this all shows us that he doesn't really have a steady stream of large income coming to him on a regular basis and that he is capable of doing virtually anything for a big payout. Someone like that can become very dangerous."

"I see what you're saying now. Yes. No. Wait. How does all that tie to a murder here in New York?"

"You're about to make history Lieutenant. Using your expertise to link a seemingly simple murder in Manhattan to an illegitimate international arms dealer."

"I am? Oh, yeah, I am. But of course Nick, you helped."

"I'm glad to be of assistance to New York's finest. Look, I think I know what has been going on here with the Finhaden case. I know it was a murder and I'm almost certain who our suspect is."

"So what's the plan Nick? How do you nail this thing down?"

"Well, Lieutenant, I have here a laundry list of names." I pulled a folded piece of paper from my jacket pocket and handed it to him.

"Alright Nick. What do you need from me?" Guild asked as he started reading down the list.

"We need everyone listed to assemble out on Long Island at Colonel MacFay's estate. We'll invite everyone to a formal dinner there at MacFay's invitation. We are only missing one piece of the jigsaw puzzle to solve this thing and I believe we can get our suspect to make some small slip up and hang himself. Or herself."

"Right."

"Between you and me, I'm leaning toward our boy Duie. It's looking more and more everyday he has the organized crime mindset, the technical know-how, the motive, and the opportunity to have done this. No real proof to charge him much less convict but that's for now. I think we can trip him up."

"It sure sounds like you're on to something. We can make a run at it."

"Alright then. You start the planning for your part and I'll get the wheels in motion on my end. I'll head out and get things started and I'll get back to you in a day or two."

19

In a matter of days Guild and I had set the stage.
One by one the names on the list were being
scratched off as they arrived at Colonel MacFay's.
Some were actually looking forward to the evening
while others needed a little persuasion to come out.
The later were issued their invitations by Lieutenant
Guild and the friendly neighborhood local law
enforcement.

Colonel MacFay's staff had set the table and
the dining room was ready for guests. Nora and I
took the liberty of setting the place cards.
Lieutenant Guild was careful to insert several of his
men in among the wait staff in the event things took
a bad turn.

Having planned on an early start we
arranged for everyone to take cocktails in the study
prior to being seated for dinner. As our guests
arrived there were staff members to direct them in.

"Mister and Missus Duie Schlusser" came
the announcement of their arrival. Then another
couple and again another.

When this small group of new arrivals began to enter the study. I stopped Sandra just inside the door. "Sandra?"

"Yes, Mr. Charles?"

"Please, call me Nick."

"Alright. Nick. What can I do for you?"

"Oh, nothing." I produced the silk handkerchief and asked her, "I thought I saw you drop this and wanted to ask if it was yours?"

Without hesitation she reached for it saying, "Oh my, yes it is. Thank you," and took it from my hand. She beamed with delight at having such a treasure returned.

"You are very welcome. I'm glad I could be of help." I stood aside and gestured for her to proceed into the library. We brought up the rear of the crowd and I stopped to close the door once inside. Everyone milled about until we all finally settled on a spot or chair.

I began the festivities. "I hope everyone had a pleasant journey here. If anyone would like a cocktail and doesn't have one yet, just head to the bar over there and help yourself. When everyone has settled in we'll start with story time before we move into the dining room."

"So Nick, what is the occasion?" asked Colonel MacFay.

"Well sir, as it turns out, Mr. Finhaden's killer is the same person responsible for the arson at the Consolidated Transcontinental plant."

With that announcement everyone stood still in their tracks and all eyes were on me. You could have heard a pin drop.

"What?" he asked, "If you know it's the same person then you know who this person is?"

"That's right, Colonel. I believe I do. And that person is here, in this room, with us now."

"Well who is it?"

"To tell the truth Colonel, I still don't know for sure but I believe I have narrowed the list down to only two, possibly three, suspects. I think we'll find out for sure very soon. Didn't you tell us you received threats before the fire?"

"Why, of course I told you. The day Macauley brought you out here with James and Nora."

"Right. You also told us the calls came directly to you on your personal unlisted private number. A number held in strict secrecy and given only to those by you."

"That is correct. The calls did all come directly to me."

"Don't you find that odd? That these calls came in on your personal, unlisted, unpublished phone?"

"Well, now that you mention it, yes I do."

"The fire and explosion, after a series of escalating threats, were nothing more than a ruse. Intended to throw suspicion onto a large unidentifiable evil organization. You see, with that threat already known, the true intentions and suspect became invisible."

"So what are you saying?" asked Nora.

"Once that link became obvious everything else, more or less, fell into place. You see, you can usually find the answers to your questions if you look at key causes. There are basically only two things that are behind murders. Passion and money. And the victim usually knew who their killer was. Or vice versa. That was the case here. This case is based on greed and the killer was well acquainted with their victim."

"Go on," said MacFay.

"Well Colonel MacFay, your daughter and her husband are also self-employed operating their own business venture."

"Yes Mr. Charles. We all know that."

"What does that have to do with all of this?" Sandra asked while standing with her hands on her hips.

"I'll get there. You and your husband, Duie here, have been operating a rather successful trade business he originated in Germany several years ago. In fact, the business was doing very well long before you two met."

"And?" Sandra replied rather tersely.

"I was able to glean some business filings and reports and learned your business has been in decline for several continuous quarters. In short, you're running out of money. You're becoming so short of money you've looked into reorganization."

"That's not true!"

"And you've resorted to exploring that because you can no longer find any source of revenue. You're over extended on margins and the original source, established by Duie back in Hamburg, the Reichsbank, will no longer extend credit to you. The same looming hyperinflation issues faced by the Reichsbank and Germany have also directly affected your business since it is primarily operating there as well."

Sandra shot a steely stare across to Duie as if this was news to her. It appeared he had also been keeping a few secrets from her.

"So now with external sources of income drying up you started to panic a little."

"None of this is true."

"Duie," I said.

Duie quickly turned in my direction, "Yes?"

"You tell me, here with everyone, have I been lying about your downturn?" Duie said nothing but dropped his gaze to the floor.

"Would you care to come clean now Duie?"

"What?"

"About Schlusser Exportieren GmbH."

"What do you mean?"

"Do you really want me to tell everyone how Schlusser Exportieren GmbH is really only a front?"

"What!?"

"Before you balk any louder ask yourself this. Would I even start going in this direction if someone hadn't done some homework? Right Lieutenant?"

"Uh, right Charles. That's right."

"You see, the NYPD uses the most modern state-of-the-art methods and resources taking a leadership position in the world as it pertains to criminal investigations. Nothing gets past these guys." Guild's chest expanded as he smiled with pride. "In fact, they just started a new Aviation Unit just this year. I think it's the first of its kind anywhere. Is that right Lieutenant?"

"Uh, yeah Nick. That's right."

"So what is it you're saying Mr. Charles?" asked Duie.

"Now with the stakes getting higher and you becoming a little more desperate you started looking at, shall we say, unconventional ways to raise revenue. The first thing to explore was insurance fraud."

"What!? Now you've gone too far," exclaimed Sandra.

"Nicky! What are you doing!?" said Nora.

"I didn't say anyone engaged in insurance fraud. You just considered it. But you're too smart to know this is a very short-sighted fix. You needed something bigger and more substantial. A long term fix. The trial run at the insurance thing was partially the reason behind the plant arson. When you saw the scrutiny given to the subsequent investigation you realized the risk verses benefit was not worth it."

"Nick, please, this is starting to sound a little over the top now," Colonel MacFay interjected.

"Please, Colonel, if you will permit only a few more minutes I will conclude this matter to your satisfaction."

Macauley spoke up, "Please Colonel. I trust Nick and his work. I know he's going somewhere with this that you will want to hear it."

"Very well then; but please get to the point."

"Sandra," I said. She focused again on me with a cold expression. "You began to think even deeper on what the solution to maintaining your lifestyle would be. Much deeper. You and Duie had several conversations about this for months. Using guilt, you enlisted Duie to help with your scheme. After all, he held the promise of a wealthy and a comfortable lifestyle independent of your father and when it came out his business was really smoke and mirrors and the money situation turned south he felt he had failed you. Then you magnified his feelings of failure. The promise of big easy money was gone after things settled down in Nicaragua."

"Not true!" she replied. "None of that is true."

"Duie?" I said. He did not reply. Turning back to Sandra, "So you began to devise a plan to inherit your father's estate. Wealth for you that would endure."

"What!?" exclaimed Colonel MacFay.

"Oh yes, Colonel. A plan was cooked up to assassinate you and for Sandra to inherit your estate. But things spiraled out of control when her greed reached its zenith. You see, she also engaged in a great deal of investigation regarding your assets and business dealings. However, what she did not count on was some of her inquiries left a paper trail. I have sources that have made these inquiries known to me. Each alone really show nothing but together you can see a pattern revealing a much bigger picture."

Sandra, raising her voice more now than before, said, "That's enough! I will not sit here and be insulted like this anymore!" and stood from her chair.

"Sit down!" answered Colonel MacFay. "Please Nick, continue." With a distinct inflection he continued, "I would like to hear this."

"The key element here was when you found the survivor clause in the original paperwork forming Consolidated Transcontinental Ventures, Incorporated. Here you found that in the event of one partner's death the other would take control of that partner's CT business interests. However, this clause would only be invoked if there were no immediate family heir. Meaning if there were no spouse or children. Extended, non-household, family members were excluded. So your sights were extended to everyone connected with CT. This only took in Nora and her father. Only two more obstacles."

"You are really reaching here Mr. Charles," said Sandra.

"Am I?"

"Nicky, please, this is driving me crazy. Tell us what you know," Nora chimed in.

"Right. Anyway, where was I? Oh yes. Does this sound about right, Duie?"

"What!?" came his wide-eyed reply.

"Right. So Sandra, it seems you planned a visit to Nora early on at the Commodore apartment. You and she were to reunite after a long separation and have a day on the town catching up. A fine thing for old friends to enjoy a fun day together. But for you this was actually more of a reconnoiter mission than a girls' day out. After you got there and Nora let you in there was a moment she had to get something from the desk. Oh yes, and her father was not there. He was here meeting privately with your father in this very room. Right Colonel?"

"Uh… yes, that is right. He was here and no one else was out here with us that day. Please continue Mr. Charles."

"When Nora sat at the desk and looked for a pen and notepad you noticed a revolver in the top right desk drawer when Nora pulled it open. Is that right, Nora?"

"That's right. I remember Sandra commented about it and I asked her if she would like to see it."

"I don't remember that" Sandra added.

"Yes you do. Let me help you out. You saw the gun and asked Nora what it was. When you did, Nora picked it up from the drawer and opened the cylinder to unload it. Having been raised as a young child out west her father taught her about guns and shooting from a very early age. She is very knowledgeable and comfortable around firearms. She unloaded the rounds from the cylinder and offered the empty gun to you. Your plan had started because you now knew Nora's fingerprints were all over the gun and ammo."

"That's right, Nick. I remember that now," said Nora.

"But you told Nora you didn't like guns and would rather not handle it."

"That's right. I did not take it or hold it. I'm afraid of guns. I told Nora I was afraid of guns," Sandra said.

"You're a liar. You are no more afraid of guns than I am. Isn't that right Duie?"

"What? Well…uh…" stammered Duie.

"That's alright old man. You needn't answer. I checked with a gun club near your home. It seems just outside of your hometown of Bennington, closer to Woodford, there are several opportunities for outdoor activities. Camping, hunting, fishing, and shooting abound there. Including a gun club both of you joined and use on a regular basis."

"How did you…" Sandra started.

"And you have a number of guns in your home. One in particular is registered to you Sandra. As I said, you are not afraid of guns. You're actually fairly proficient with them."

"Okay, I own a gun. I'm still afraid of them and I'm not a very good shot. And how does this all relate to what happened to Nora's father anyway?"

"There were a number of discrepancies and deficiencies with the police investigation. I had the opportunity to review all of the related files and returned to the apartment for one last check of the scene. That day I went to the Commodore alone. They had maintained the apartment as a police crime scene and nothing had been disturbed since the day in question. This is all documented and can easily be verified through Commodore corporate and police department documentation. Oh, one small correction, I wasn't exactly alone. Asta came with me."

Sandra asked in an exasperated tone , "And who is Asta?"

"Asta is a Wire Fox Terrier and my partner. After spending a while going over the apartment

159

again I took careful note of the lock on the entrance door. With the help of extra light, I noted marks and scratches in the lock's keyway that none of the others in the hallway had. Without question, someone picked the lock to gain entry to the apartment. The killer did not use a key because the killer did not need one. Duie? Didn't you at one time work in the locksmithing trade?"

"Well, yes, but…"

"Thank you. In fact, you learned that skill while serving in the German Army as a special operative training with the Jagkommandos."

"How did you—"

"Asta was paying particular attention to a spot on the bedroom door frame about two or three feet from the floor and on the latch side. When I looked closer, and with better light, I noticed the spot was slightly darker than the surrounding area. The crème colored paint was a little discolored. It turned out this was residue from a fired gun."

Colonel MacFay asked, "Mr. Charles, are you telling us someone fired a gun while standing in the doorway to the bedroom?"

"Yes sir. Actually, someone fired a pistol while in a classic braced barricade kneeling position. A shooting position taught and practiced at police shooting ranges and gun club ranges. In this very stable braced position the back of the shooters hand and the gun are in very close proximity to the wooden door frame. When the gun fired minute gunshot residue left the gun and deposited on everything close by. The shooter's hands, clothes, and the door frame. In short, there is physical

160

evidence proving someone fired a gun into the bedroom while kneeling at the bedroom door. Did Sandra get you to do this Duie?"

"No! I mean, I have no idea what you're talking about. I haven't shot anyone. No!" he answered.

"We also have the scene as recorded that day by the police. The official reports show they initially thought it to be a suicide. The sketches and photographs show Mr. Finhaden was lying on his back in the bed. He had been shot in the right temple and his gun was lying on the floor next to the bed. It seemed he used the gun with his right hand and then the right arm fell to the side of the bed and the gun fell from his hand to the floor. All staged."

Nora began to look more anguished as the description of her father was given and she suddenly changed to an appearance of extreme soberness. "Nicky, did you say he was shot on the right side? With the right hand? The gun was on the floor to his right side?"

"Yes."

"I saw that when I walked in, but I was so upset then it didn't register. My father was left-handed. None of that makes sense. Why would someone left-handed do that?"

"Further making my point. Thank you, Nora. In fact, he was not shot by that gun. He did not shoot himself. When the police examined the gun, they found something very unusual. You see, the gun is a brand-new Smith & Wesson Military & Police Model of 1905 K-Frame revolver; serial

161

#544588. It is chambered for the .38 Special round. It was manufactured and shipped out to Mr. Finhaden last year. When they opened the cylinder, they found it was loaded with five rounds of live unfired .38 Special ammunition and a single fired brass case in the chamber under the hammer."

"Please, Mr. Charles. Get to the point," Sandra said in an extremely peremptory tone.

"Gladly. The empty shell casing was a .32-20 round."

"What?" came Colonel MacFay.

"Yes sir, a .32-20. The same caliber you have in your desk."

"Now, what are you implying?"

"I'm not implying anything Colonel. I'm merely stating fact at this time. The round recovered from Mr. Finhaden was also a .32 caliber bullet. This was confirmed by the medical examiner's office and then again at the NYPD crime lab." I continued after a very brief pause with, "Colonel, you will remember the last time I was out here and needed to use your telephone?"

"Yes, I do remember."

"When I did I too saw your gun in a desk drawer when I needed a pen and paper. Seeing that it was marked on the barrel as a .32-20 and knowing about the oddball shell in the Finhaden gun, I borrowed it for a while. You'll remember that too. Nora and I went out back for some target shooting."

"Yes. I remember," said MacFay. "I told you where to walk to target shoot. Did you think I had anything to do with his death?"

"Not really, but you do know everything has to be looked at and yes, you did provide the gun and place to shoot. In fact, those gestures further made me believe you had nothing to do with the murder. If you had been involved, and used that gun, you certainly wouldn't have let me have it. While Nora and I were down there I did fire two rounds I recovered for comparison and later returned the gun to the desk drawer when we finished. I also made notes to identify that gun for future reference."

"Now hold on. How did you manage to fire two bullets you could pick up and take back to town?" asked Sandra rather indignantly.

"Water. You can shoot into water and get them back almost in perfect condition" replied Duie.

"Correct. Thank you Duie. That is exactly what I did. I actually fired into a large bucket filled with water and placed in shallow water at the creek bank."

"So that's what you were doing?" asked Nora.

"That is what I was doing."

"Go on," the Colonel said.

"The two rounds I fired were compared to the recovered bullet. All three bullets have been confirmed to have been fired from the same gun."

"What!?"

"Specifically, the murder weapon in question is in fact a Colt Police Positive Special revolver with serial number 47731 manufactured in 1911. It is similar in size and function to the Smith & Wesson and, just as the Smith & Wesson, is very popular in police use. Both Colt and Smith & Wesson, make these similar models in both the .38 and .32-20 calibers. And this particular one is registered to you Colonel."

"If you know it was my gun used to kill him but don't think I was behind it, then who used my gun to kill him?"

"Sandra?" I asked.

"What!? I haven't killed anyone! How would I get father's gun, go to New York and shoot someone, and then drive all the way back here and put it back in the desk?"

"I know you have recently taken up the shooting sports and learning about guns. However, you still have a way to go. For example, your father's Colt and Nora's father's Smith & Wesson look like the same gun at first glance and to the uninitiated. Smith and Wesson makes their model in both calibers. It is even possible to insert a .32-20 round into the .38 Special cylinder and close it. However, I would never try to fire it. Bad things would happen."

"Again, what does all this have to do with me?"

"The night Nora and I walked to the Yale Club she said to me she thought she saw you walking along the Grand Central side of the street back toward the Commodore. She then dismissed it. In fact, Nora did see you walking back to the Commodore as we made our way to dinner. While we enjoyed the evening at the Yale Club, and other places, you and Duie killed your best friend's father." Nora was becoming more visibly upset. She was close to crying as she listened.

"You're mad Mr. Charles!" yelled Sandra.

"Am I? In order to draw less attention, the two of you decided to walk to the hotel and from different directions. You entered the building individually and took different elevators. No one in the hotel and none of the elevator operators could recall seeing a couple enter together during that time frame. You were even careful to not be spotted standing at the Finhaden apartment door together. One couple, or rather other denizens residing there year-round, stated they saw an unknown man standing at Finhaden's door alone when they stepped off the elevator and walked to their suite. They know everyone on their floor and take note of new and unknown faces. Do you remember hearing the elevator stop and the doors opening, Duie?"

"Why ask me? It wasn't me."

"Yes, it was. I personally spoke to the neighbors who spotted you. The Pattersons residing in Suite 722. And one elevator operator who can identify you. Shall we ask them again? On a witness stand perhaps?"

"What?"

"You finished raking and picking the lock and then simply walked away. When you left, you took the stairs so no one would see you leave the building. You certainly didn't want to take the chance of an elevator operator remembering you coming and going."

"You can't prove anything you've said. You're guessing at all of this," said Sandra.

"You, Sandra, had borrowed your father's gun, albeit without his knowledge or permission, not wanting to take the risk of having your own gun remotely connected to the crime. You had it with you the night Nora saw you walking across the street. From the stairway at the end of the hall you saw Duie complete his task and head for the opposite stairway. After a few minutes you simply sauntered to the unlocked door and slipped right in quickly and unnoticed. When you realized you were safely inside and could hear Mr. Finhaden sleeping down the hall you moved into position. By now it was very late in the evening and he was sleeping heavily. You placed your purse on the desk and pulled the revolver out. Leaving your coat and purse in the parlor you even slipped off your shoes to make your steps even stealthier. You made your way to the bedroom door and lightly pushed it open just enough to see Mr. Finhaden lying in the bed. The ambient light of a very dim night stand light was just enough to make out the silhouette of his head. You then assumed a one knee kneeling position and braced your gun hand against the door frame. You carefully squeezed the trigger, as you've practiced at your gun club range, and 'bang'. You sat in the dark and subsequent silence for several minutes. Waiting and listening for any responses to the fired shot. You heard nothing."

"Mr. Charles, this all sounds like a fine story but where is any proof. You actually have nothing to back up any of this," said Duie.

"Sandra walked back to the desk and could now turn on a lamp. She opened the desk drawer

166

and with gloved hands picked up Finhaden's gun being very careful not to disturb any of Nora's fingerprints. She was able to work the cylinder release and removed one of the six rounds. In the place of the removed round she took the fired casing out of the Colonel's gun and inserted into Finhaden's." I looked directly at Sandra and continued, "Although the desk lamp was on, the light was very dim and you didn't notice the difference in calibers. The spent case went into the chamber you just emptied and you closed the cylinder. All seemed to be going as planned. Had you used another .38 Special your plan may have actually worked. You were so careful in handling the gun Nora's fingerprints were still found on the cylinder, frame, and even on the trigger."

"What plan? I still don't know what you're talking about." Sandra replied.

"Then to return the gun to your father the two of you came up with that bogus excuse of a side trip to the beaches. You had to leave for home in order to go to New York to kill Finhaden and then you had to get the gun back here."

"Mr. Charles, this has all been very interesting and I appreciate your time and interest in this case, but can you please connect the dots for us. You still haven't told us anything or displayed anything that would carry the day in a court of law," said Colonel MacFay.

"Right you are Colonel. In summary the master plan had built in residuals. After careful consideration, Sandra and Duie settled on plans to inherit the entire business empire. All they had to do was to kill Mr. Finhaden then frame Nora for the murder or lacking that, kill her. Then after you took control of the entire business empire she would get Duie to kill you too."

"Mr. Charles! This is about enough!" exclaimed Duie.

"Sandra?"

"What?"

"Do you remember just before we walked into this room?"

"Yes. Why?"

"The dainty silk soie handkerchief I returned to you?"

"Yes?" she answered slowly. In a very aloof and condescending tone she continued, "I have those custom made in Paris. The design is an original I submitted with the first order."

"I know. You can't find this handkerchief anywhere in New York stores."

"That's correct," she said.

"But I did find that one on top of Mr. Finhaden's desk mixed in with the other items."

"What!?"

"Yes. With the embroidered monogram of 'SMS' for Sandra MacFay Schlusser. It seems that when you first got there and were still stumbling around in the dark you set your purse on the desk in order to have a stable platform to find and pull the gun out. When you drew the gun from your purse it snagged and pulled the handkerchief out with it. Once it cleared the purse and you were focused on walking to the bedroom door it fell from the gun

168

and onto the floor or desktop. You never noticed it and left it behind."

"That's still too thin."

Colonel MacFay interjected, "Mr. Charles. Do you have anything concrete to offer or are you just grasping at straws here?"

"I'm getting there. Please allow me just another minute."

"Very well. But make your point please."

Turning my focus back to Sandra I continued with, "Is it too thin? I found your milliner and was able to trace this piece with a specific order. They don't stock this item but do maintain records of their regular customers, especially high-end orders and regular repeat customers. I ran this down when I first showed it to Nora and asked if it was hers. I never told her where I found it and she told me she had no idea whose it was. So tell me Duie, are you ready to face a murder charge for this?"

"I didn't kill anyone! I have nothing to do with this. The whole thing was her idea!"

"Shut up Duie! This is what he wants!" yelled Sandra.

"Sandra, what are you saying?" shouted Nora.

"Duie, if you keep supporting Sandra's lies you'll be facing the chair too. She'll probably even say you killed him and put the whole thing on you. Oh yeah, I almost forgot. I checked and found the truck used in the New Jersey mill bombing was reported stolen the day before to your hometown police department."

"This was all her idea! I—"

Sandra now worked up into a lather yelled back, "What does that prove, Mr. Charles!?"

"A car was also seen leaving the property only minutes before the explosion. A car bearing a Vermont license plate, number 62-354. The guard, thinking the timing of the departure was unusual, jotted it down in his notebook. And one more thing. The same night Nora and her father arrived in New York where Macauley had me meet them with him, the two of you arranged to meet me at my home but you missed me. I spent most of the night somewhere else. I also found the same lock picking scratches on my door that were on Finhaden's door. I don't know if the two of you found what you were looking for in my apartment, but it doesn't matter now. It took me a little time to make that connection until we got the information from the plant guard. Duie, this is your plate and car. It seems you two had been planning this scheme for a very long time. What's it going to be?"

"I want a lawyer. I'll tell you everything, but I want my lawyer first. I am not going down for a murder charge! She's crazy!"

"I think we're past that Duie."

"You big mouth idiot! I'll kill you too!" Sandra screamed as she drew a pistol from her coat pocket. She was out of control with anger.

I said, "Sandra, you don't want to do this."

Looking in my direction she answered, "Why not? I've got nothing to lose now. The big famous detective figured out I shot Nora's father. The chair won't be any worse if I shoot anyone

170

else! No, Mr. Charles you're wrong. I do want to do this." She turned her attention back to Duie. "You sniveling idiot. You've ruined everything. But you'll never have the chance to mess things up ever again!" She slowly raised her gun higher as though she was savoring the moment. "You've ruined everything!"

"Sandra!" yelled out Nora. Sandra snapped her head around. I pulled my revolver out unnoticed.

"Sandra!" I yelled loudly.

Confused, she turned back, looking directly at the business end of my barrel with her gun still pointing at Duie. "Sandra. Lower the muzzle now. If I repeat myself I will shoot you." I followed up with a very loud, "Now!"

She briefly looked as if she was weighing her options but lowered the muzzle toward the floor. Guild and all his men drew and took aim now. "Sandra?"

"Yes Mr. Charles."

"Sandra, there are now several guns trained on you. Drop the gun on the floor. If you do anything other than that you will not survive. Do you understand what I'm telling you?" Sandra's hand relaxed and opened. Then came the distinct thud of two pounds of Smith and Wesson revolver hitting the floor. Everyone re-holstered and Guild stepped up and took her by the arm.

When Guild secured Sandra, I started to re-holster my gun when the sound of one lone shot rang out. Poor Duie was holding his right hand with his left bleeding profusely and yelling out in pain.

Nora was holding her little M-Frame Lady Smith .22 and a derringer was lying on the floor at Duie's feet.

"I'm disappointed in you gentlemen." Looking directly at me Nora smugly followed up with, "I bet you're glad I came along today."

"I can't argue that one," I replied. "I guess your father did teach you how to shoot."

Guild's men quickly finished handcuffing Sandra as well as securing Duie. "Wait! I didn't kill anyone. I didn't do this," he continued, even with a new hole in his right hand. Sandra continued to kick and scream in a rage all the way out the door.

"Sorry buddy. You're in this up to your nostrils. A judge and jury are gonna' have to sort this out. Let's go" replied Guild. He then paused and turned back saying, "And, uh, thanks Miss Finhaden. Thanks a lot. Bye now."

She replied, "Oh, anytime Lieutenant. I was glad to do it."

"Well there are your killers. Sandra and Duie. They cooked up a fairly elaborate scheme in order to kill their way to inheriting your business empire. They killed your father, and were planning on killing her own father too, for money. And you Nora; they were going to frame you for killing your father and if that didn't work would follow up with a slightly modified version of the scheme where they would wind up killing you too. Sandra's state of mind, intentions, and actions reveal one of the most truculent examples of a single individual I've personally known. I'm just glad you only shot

172

Duie's hand and didn't go ahead and kill both of them."

"Oh Sandra, how did all this happen?" said Nora, although Sandra had just been taken from the room and could not hear her. She then looked at me. "Thanks for not telling me everything you knew when you knew it. If I had known the details of the case like you did, I may have killed them. I guess you knew that."

"Mr. Charles, I don't know what to say," said Colonel MacFay.

"No need to say anything Colonel. I'm glad to help. Oh, and I'll also be submitting my bill to your attorney."

"You know where my office is," smiled Macauley.

"Let's get 'em back to the city boys," said Guild to his crew. This wasn't really necessary. They were already headed for the door.

20

A few days later most of the loose ends had been dealt with. Lawyers were cleaning up the last few legal entanglements for Colonel MacFay and Nora. It was time for Nora to head back to Poughkeepsie and finish out the year. Although she had lost her father and Colonel MacFay, his daughter, they were making plans to put the pieces back together. Nora would soon be a graduate of Vassar and a major player in a massive business enterprise. It was the start of the next chapter in her life.

A few days after the excitement, I received a surprise telephone call from Nora. It was a very welcome surprise. "Hello?" I said.

"Nicky? It's Nora."

"Nora!? Well. How've you been? It's so good to hear your voice again."

"You too Nicky. I called to ask you a question."

"Okay. Go ahead. Anything for you."

"Nicky?"

"Yes."

"Nicky, my graduation from Vassar is coming up soon."

"Yes?"

"Well, since my father is, well, no longer here, I really have no one here to come with me to commencement."

"Yes."

"Nicky, would you be my escort for graduation?"

"When is it?"

"It's scheduled for Tuesday, June twelve."

"Oh Nora, I'm sorry. The Yankees are playing the White Sox that day."

"Nicky!"

"Who could pass up watching Gehrig and the Babe?"

"Nicky! You've got to be kidding!?"

"I am. I'd love to be your escort. Count me in."

"Good. Now, I will be going back to San Francisco for my birthday. I'm taking father back to California for his funeral too. But I have told all my friends and family I had to make it back here for June though."

"Oh, okay."

"So, I'll be back and see you there in about a month, okay?"

"Sure. Just call my office when you get back and we'll work the details out then."

"Okay Nicky. Take care of yourself and we'll talk then. I have to go now. Bye."

"Goodbye Nora." As I hung the phone up I had the feeling we would not make that date. Since I actually looked forward to seeing her again I concentrated on work to put it out of my mind.

Formal charges had been filed against
Sandra and Duie Schlusser by the DA's office and
life in Manhattan was slipping back to its old,
familiar, and dull state. They would be out of
circulation for a very long time since they also had
the arson charge to deal with in New Jersey as well.
It even looked like the Federal Government might
take a swing at them over the Nicaragua affair. The
poor girl remained supercilious up to the very end. I
hope for her sake she can get beyond that.

The Finhaden murder case preliminary
hearing was scheduled and the case was winding
down for me. Yesterday my secretary told me we
had ten new calls from potential clients. Business
was good. It has been for some time, but most are
domestic cases. I've all but sworn those off. Every
one of them, without fail, are trouble no one needs.
People turn crazy in those cases. When I see these,
it makes me glad I never got married. The buzzer on
my intercom sounded. "Yes Miss Landers," I
answered.

"Mr. Charles, I have a call asking for you."

"Take a number and tell them I'll call back.
I'm with another client right now," although we
both knew I wasn't.

"Mr. Charles?"

"Yes Carol?"

"She told me to tell you it's Miss Finhaden.
Letty Finhaden."

"Put the call through."

After a click or two I heard, "Nicky?"

"Yes, Miss Finhaden."

176

"Nicky, I'm also in need of someone to escort me and father back to California and generally work as my bodyguard. I just realized I will be making that cross-country trip all alone. Do you know anyone you would recommend?"

"I'm sorry Miss Finhaden. I just can't think of a single person I could recommend for such an important job as that."

"Alright then, you're hired. You may drive up and pick me up Monday."

"You slay me Nora. I'll need a little more time than that to consider the job offer. I will have to let you know when I can close the shop."

"You have my number Nicky. Call me when you're ready."

After I hung up the phone I walked to the outer office. "Carol?"

"Yes?"

"How would you feel about a job transfer to San Francisco?"

"What?"

"We'll talk about it later."

21

Come Monday morning I found myself in her neighborhood and stopped at the bus station to use the payphone.

"Hello?"

"Nora. It's Nick.

"Nick?"

"Yes, it's me. I thought I would call this morning to double check on that job offer."

"Oh yes. Well what did you decide?"

"I think I'm ready to go when you are. You know I still need my secretary. She'll need a job offer and a transfer too."

"Do you have my address up here?"

"I'm not sure. What is it?"

"When you get to the campus just come to the Raymond House. Anyone there can direct you to me. I was so hoping to board in the new Cushing House this year but it wasn't meant to be. It was just built last year and has all the most up-to-date modern amenities."

"Well I'm sure with your financial situation and Colonel MacFay managing the businesses you'll be able to buy or build whatever you like when you get back to San Francisco."

"I guess that's true. Well, hang up and drive on up."

"I'm at the Poughkeepsie bus station now."

"Bus station? Now?"

"I just stopped here to phone. I'm driving."

"Oh. Okay."

"You get packed and I'll be along in about half an hour. Then we'll head back to New York and get you and your father on a westbound train."

"Well, that's kinda' sudden. I don't know if I can be ready that soon."

"Look Missy, I'm here. Get ready because we're leaving."

"Well... alright then."

I hung up and left the bus station for the school. After a short but scenic ride through the countryside the campus came into view. As I was easing down the streets of the campus I stopped along the curb near a couple of young ladies strolling along a walkway. "Excuse me ladies!"

They stopped and looked in my direction. "Yes sir?"

"Yes. Well, could you direct me to Raymond House? I'm looking for a Miss Nora Finhaden. She might be known as Lettie too. I'm to escort her back to her home in San Francisco."

"Oh, Lettie, yes we know her. We live in Raymond House too. It's just one block up. Turn right and it's on the right."

"Thank you ladies. Have a lovely day." Asta, sitting in the passenger seat, yipped a thank you to them as well.

179

I turned the corner and there she was. Sitting on a trunk with two smaller bags near her. She presented the image of a homeless person waiting for the kindness of a stranger. As I made the turn and saw her I arced across the center line and then back to the curb stopping abruptly next to her. When the car stopped she looked up and Asta leapt from the car. Nora's focus quickly went from the car to the charging terrier. He jumped into her lap and attacked her with a barrage of dog kisses. I was relieved to see she loved dogs and didn't mind. I guess Asta already knew that before I did.

"Asta!" she exclaimed.

"Excuse me miss. Could you direct me to Raymond House? I'm looking for a Miss Lettie Finhaden."

"Well sir, I'm not really sure where it is. If you will, I could get in and possibly help you find her."

"That sounds like a fine idea. Good thing for you Asta likes you."

"Oh?"

"You do remember we talked about this once before? He can sense if someone is a good person."

"You really think so?"

"There's no question about it. It's not just Asta either. Dogs in general. If someone hates dogs they know it. And I think people who hate dogs have something wrong with them."

"Well, being from the wild west, I love animals and was raised having dogs too. So, do I pass the test?"

"Yes ma'am, you absolutely do. Asta says you can come with us."

I loaded her baggage into the car and we were on our way back to New York. Rumbling down the open road outside of town we started into the crux of things.

"So we're taking your father back to San Francisco?"

"Yes Nicky. I really do need your help traveling with him all the way back across the country. I've given this a lot of thought and I would have never survived the past weeks without you."

"That's nice and all but…"

"No buts. It's true. Plus I like you."

"Well…"

"A lot."

"Well Nora. I have something I've been wanting to tell you too."

"Would you like to tell me again when we get to San Francisco and meet with Father Cariss?"

"What?"

"When we meet with Father Cariss. He will be conducting father's funeral mass you know."

"Oh, that. Oh. Alright then."

"What did you think I meant?"

"Well, uh, I'm not sure. I mean, yes, the funeral."

"Nicky?"

"What?"

"When this is all over…"

"Yes?"

"Would you like to go with me to talk with Father Cariss again?"

181

"Again?"

"Yes Nicky, again?"

"About what?"

"And you're supposed to be the great detective Nick Charles. Did you forget this is a Leap Year?"

"Leap Year? What are you saying Nora?" Although at this point in the conversation I knew darn well where this was going.

"Nicky. I might as well put this out there right now before you leave New York and find yourself in California. How would you feel about making our partnership permanent?"

"Permanent?"

"Do you remember, 'Gather ye rosebuds while ye may'?"

"Oh, yes. That first day together in the car. The day you became Nora."

"That's right. That is the opening line of the poem. Now I would like to cite the ending."

"Alright."

"Then be not coy, but use your time, and, while ye may, go marry."

"What?"

"Nicky, I'm asking if you would marry me."

"It's a good thing this is a leap year or I would think you were a forward young lady."

"There's nothing wrong with women asking men to marry. It's 1928. Women won the vote at the beginning of this decade and we're now in a new modern era."

"So you're saying men and women are now equal?"

"Yes I am."

"To tell the truth, I guess you're right."

"I know I'm right. I believe in seizing the day. And life is short. When you see something you want why waste time? 'For having lost but once your prime, you may forever tarry'."

"Oh, don't get me wrong. I'll marry you. I'm just quite a bit slower and shyer than you when it comes to this."

"I know. You're always the gentleman. I'm not."

"No ma'am, you are no gentleman, indeed."

"I'm glad you noticed."

Made in the USA
Columbia, SC
17 June 2025

59503176R00109